"What Exactly Do You Want, Colt?"

"That's easy," he said. "I want what's mine."

What was his? She knew he didn't mean that he wanted her, so he was talking about her kids. Her babies.

Fear coiled around her heart and made breathing almost impossible. But where she might try to run and hide to protect herself—to safeguard her children she was willing to walk into hell itself.

She watched him through the car window, and when he opened her door to help her out, she looked into his eyes and said, "You can't have them."

* * *

Double the Trouble is part of the #1 bestselling miniseries from Harlequin Desire— Billionaires & Babies: Powerful men... wrapped around their babies' little fingers.

* * *

If you're on Twitter, tell us what you think of Harlequin Desire! #harlequindesire

Dear Reader,

I love writing "secret baby" books. Writing about twins is just twice the fun! And throw in one of the Kings of California and the fun quotient goes through the roof.

In *Double the Trouble,* you'll meet Colton King, a man who lives life on the edge. He's a daredevil, an extreme sports enthusiast—until he finds out he's also the father of eight-month-old twins. That's when the *real* extreme adventure begins!

The mother of his children, Penny Oaks, had her reasons for not telling Colt about the twins. But now that he knows the truth, he's determined to be a part of his kids' lives—whether Penny likes it or not.

I really hope you enjoy Colt and Penny's story. Please stop by my Facebook page and let me know what you think!

Happy Reading,

Maureen

DOUBLE
THE TROUBLE

—

MAUREEN CHILD

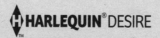

Recycling programs
for this product may
not exist in your area.

ISBN-13: 978-0-373-73302-6

DOUBLE THE TROUBLE

Printed in U.S.A.

Books by Maureen Child

Harlequin Desire

*King's Million-Dollar Secret #2083
  One Night, Two Heirs #2096
*Ready for King's Seduction #2113
*The Temporary Mrs. King #2125
*To Kiss a King #2137
  Gilded Secrets #2168
  Up Close and Personal #2179
  An Outrageous Proposal #2191
*The King Next Door #2209
  Rumor Has It #2240
  The Lone Star Cinderella #2258
*Her Return to King's Bed #2269
*Double the Trouble #2289

Silhouette Desire

ΩScorned by the Boss #1816
ΩSeduced by the Rich Man #1820
ΩCaptured by the Billionaire #1826
 *Bargaining for King's Baby #1857
 *Marrying for King's Millions #1862
 *Falling for King's Fortune #1868

 High-Society Secret Pregnancy #1879
 Baby Bonanza #1893
 An Officer and a Millionaire #1915
 Seduced Into a Paper Marriage #1946
*Conquering King's Heart #1965
*Claiming King's Baby #1971
*Wedding at King's
  Convenience #1978
*The Last Lone Wolf #2011
 Claiming Her Billion-Dollar
  Birthright #2024
*Cinderella & the CEO #2043
 Under the Millionaire's
  Mistletoe #2056
  "The Wrong Brother"
 Have Baby, Need
  Billionaire #2059

ΩReasons for Revenge
 *Kings of California

Other titles by this author
available in ebook format.

MAUREEN CHILD

writes for the Harlequin Desire line and can't imagine a better job. Being able to indulge your love for romance, as well as being able to spin stories just the way you want them told is, in a word, perfect.

A seven-time finalist for the prestigious Romance Writers of America RITA® Award, Maureen is the author of more than one hundred romance novels. Her books regularly appear on the bestseller lists and have won several awards, including a Prism, a National Readers' Choice Award, a Colorado Romance Writers Award of Excellence and a Golden Quill.

One of her books, *The Soul Collector,* was made into a CBS TV movie starring Melissa Gilbert, Bruce Greenwood and Ossie Davis. If you look closely, in the last five minutes of the movie, you'll spot Maureen, who was an extra in the last scene.

Maureen believes that laughter goes hand in hand with love, so her stories are always filled with humor. The many letters she receives assures her that her readers love to laugh as much as she does.

Maureen Child is a native Californian, but has recently moved to the mountains of Utah. She loves a new adventure, though the thought of having to deal with snow for the first time is a little intimidating.

To Harlequin Desire readers everywhere.
Thank you so much for embracing the
Kings of California—and me. You make it possible
for me to do what I most love to do. Tell stories.

One

Colton King never saw the fist that slammed into his jaw.

He shook his head to clear it, then blocked the next punch before it could land. The furious man who'd stormed into Colt's office only moments before took a step back and ground out, "You had that coming."

"What the hell?" Colt dropped his packed duffel bag to the floor. "Had it coming?"

Colt did a fast mental review and came up empty. He didn't know this man and he couldn't think of a single other person who wanted to hit him—at the moment. His always-temporary relationships with women invariably ended amicably. Heck, even he and his twin brother, Connor, hadn't had a good argument in weeks.

Yeah, he'd had angry clients show up at the Laguna Beach, California, offices of King's Extreme Adventures if they didn't find the monster waves they'd been promised. Or if the dead man's run on a mountain was closed due to avalanche.

Colton and Connor arranged adventure vacations for the wealthy adrenaline junkies of the world. So, sure, there had been more than a few times when a customer was mad enough to cause a scene. But not one of them had ever punched him. Before now.

So the question was, "Who the hell are you?"

"I called security!" A woman announced from the doorway.

Colt didn't even glance at Linda, the admin he and Connor shared. "Thanks. Go get Connor."

"On it," she said, then vanished.

"Calling security won't change anything," the guy who had just punched him said flatly. "You'll still be a selfish bastard."

"Okay," Colt muttered. Not the first time he'd heard that, either. But a little context would be helpful. "You want to tell me what's going on here?"

"That's what I'd like to know." Connor stepped into the room to take a stand beside his twin.

Colt was glad to have him there, though he could have taken the guy who'd gotten in one lucky sucker punch. But probably not good business to have a fistfight here in the office, and having Connor around would help him leash his temper. Besides, fighting wouldn't give him the answers he wanted. "You took your best shot. Now tell me *why*."

"My name is Robert Oaks."

Oaks. Long-buried memories raced through Colt's mind in a blinding rush. A ball of ice dropped into the pit of his stomach and his body went utterly still. He studied the stranger glaring at him and in those narrowed green eyes, he saw…familiarity.

Damn it.

The last time he'd looked into eyes like those had been nearly two years ago. At the end of a week in Vegas that should have been ordinary and instead had been…amazing. One specific memory rose up in his mind and Colt wished to hell he could wipe it away, but he'd never been able to pull that off. The morning after he and Penny Oaks had gotten married in a tacky chapel on the strip. The morning when he'd told her they'd be getting a divorce—right before thanking her for a fun week and then leaving her in the hotel room they'd shared.

He didn't want to think about that day. But hard to avoid that now, with the man who had to be her brother standing in front of him.

Robert Oaks nodded slowly as he saw realization dawn on Colt's face. "Good. At least you remember."

"Remember what?" Connor demanded.

"Nothing." He wasn't getting into this with Connor. Not right now, anyway.

"Oh, *nothing*. That's great." Oaks shook his head in disgust. "Just what I expected."

Anger stirred. Whatever was once between him and Penny was just that. Between the two of them. He wasn't interested in what her brother thought. "Why are you here? What do you want?"

"I want you to do the right thing," Robert snapped. "But I doubt you will." His fist bunched. "So I thought punching you would be enough. It wasn't."

Impatience stirred and twisted in the anger still balled in Colt's guts. He had a KingJet waiting to fly him to

Sicily. He had places to go. Things to do. And damned if he'd waste one more minute with Robert Oaks.

"Why don't you quit dancing around and get to it. Why are you here?"

"Because my sister's in the hospital."

"Hospital?" Something inside Colt lurched unsteadily. Instantly, memories shifted, his mind filling with images of another hospital, the cold green walls, the grim gray linoleum and the stench of fear and antiseptic flavoring every breath.

For a second or two, he felt as though there was a weight on his chest, dragging him back into a past he never wanted to visit again. Deliberately, he pushed away from the blackness at the edges of his mind and fought his way back to the present. Pushing one hand through his hair, Colt focused his gaze on Penny's brother and waited.

"My sister had an appendectomy yesterday," Robert told him.

Relief that it wasn't something more serious was a small, slim thread winding its way through the tangled mass inside him. "Is she okay?"

Robert snorted a derisive laugh. "Yeah, she's fine. Except, you know, for worrying about how she's going to pay the hospital bill. And worrying about her twins. *Your* twins."

All of the air left the room.

Colt knew that because he couldn't draw a breath.

"My—" He shook his head while he tried to get a grip on what Penny's younger brother was telling him. But how the hell did you make sense of something like *that* coming at you out of the blue? What the hell was he supposed to do? Say? Think?

Colt scrubbed both hands across his face, forced one shaky breath into his lungs and finally managed to say, "*Twins?* Penny had a baby?"

"Two," Robert corrected, and looked from Colt to Connor and back again. "Looks like twins run in your family."

"And she didn't tell him?" Connor sounded as stunned as Colt felt.

Fury rose up and nearly choked him. She had never said a damn word. She'd been pregnant and hadn't told him. She'd delivered two children and hadn't told him.

He had *children?*

That weight was back on his chest again but this time he ignored it.

"Where are they?" The demand was short and sharp.

Robert looked at him warily and Colt knew that his expression must have mirrored the anger erupting inside.

"My fiancée and I have been taking care of them."

Them. Colt was the father of twins and he knew nothing about them. How was that even possible? He'd always been careful. But apparently, his mind taunted, not careful enough.

A small voice in the back of his mind whispered that this might all be a lie. That Penny could have told her brother a lie. That the babies weren't really *his.* But even as he considered that possibility, he dismissed it. That would have been too easy, and Colt knew better than most that there was nothing *easy* about any of this.

"A boy and a girl, if you're interested."

Colt's head snapped up and his gaze narrowed on Robert. *A boy and a girl.* He had two kids. Hell, he didn't know how he was supposed to feel. The only thing he was sure of at the moment was that his children's mother had some explaining to do.

"Damn straight I'm interested. Now tell me what hospital Penny's in."

He got all the information from Robert, including the man's cell number and his address. When building security arrived, Colt sent them away. He wasn't going to press charges against Penny's brother—the guy was pissed and defending his family. Colton would have done the same. But once Robert had left, Colt released some of his fury by kicking his duffel bag across the room.

Connor leaned against the doorjamb. "So, trip to Sicily is off?"

Colt was supposed to be in the air right now, heading for Mount Etna to try out a new BASE jumping spot. It's what he did—searching out the most dangerous, most awe-inspiring sport sites for their ever-growing client list.

But now, he had a different sort of adrenaline burst waiting for him. Colt slanted his twin a hard look. "Yeah, it's off."

"And you're a father."

"Looks like it."

He sounded calm, didn't he? He wasn't, though. There were too many emotions, too many thoughts crowding his mind for him to even separate one from the other. A *father.* There were two babies in the world because of *him,* and he'd had no idea until a few minutes ago. How was that even possible? Shouldn't he have *felt* something? Shouldn't he have damn well been *told* that he was a father?

Colt shook his head, still trying to wrap his mind around it. He couldn't. Hell, no kid deserved to have him for a father. He knew that. Rubbing the center of his chest to try to ease the ache settled there, Colt blew out a breath. How was he supposed to be feeling? Anger tangled with sheer terror, then twisted into a tight knot that iced over and left him feeling cold to the bone.

"And you were gonna tell me about this when?"

Colt gaped at his twin. "Seriously? I just found out myself, remember?"

"I'm not talking about the twins—I'm talking about their mother."

"Nothing to tell." Lies, he thought. Lies. Truth was, there was plenty to tell, just nothing he wanted to talk about. It was the only time in his life Colt had kept something from his twin. He still couldn't explain why. Colt shoved one hand through his hair. "It was the convention in Vegas nearly two years ago."

"You met her there?"

Colt stalked across the room and picked up the duffel he'd packed for his now-canceled trip to Sicily. Slinging it over his shoulder, he turned to face his brother. "I don't want to talk about this now, okay?"

If he didn't get out of there in the next ten seconds, he was going to blow. Temper boiling, it was all he could do to hold it together.

"Too bad," Connor said shortly. "I just found out I'm an uncle. So tell me about this woman."

His twin wasn't going to let this go and Colt knew it. Hell, if the situation was reversed, he'd be demanding answers, too, so he couldn't really blame him. Didn't make this any easier, though.

"Not much to say," he ground out, teeth gritted. "I met her at the extreme sports convention. We spent the week together and then—"

"Then?"

Colt blew out a breath. "We got married."

If he hadn't been in such a foul mood the look on his twin's face would have made Colt laugh hysterically. He'd never seen Connor so shocked. Of course, why wouldn't he be? Colt felt pretty much as if someone had knocked him over the head with a two-by-four, himself.

"You got *married?*" Connor pushed away from the doorjamb and stalked into the room. "And you didn't bother to tell me?"

"It lasted, like, a *minute*," Colt said. Even now he couldn't believe that he'd surrendered so deeply to the passion he'd found with Penny that he'd actually married her. He hadn't said anything to Connor because he hadn't even been able to explain to himself what he'd done.

Shaking his head, he turned and looked out the window at the ocean beyond the glass. Surfers rode their boards toward shore. Tourists strolled along the beach, snapping pictures as they went, and farther out on the water, sailboats skimmed the surface, bright sails fluttering in the wind.

The world was going on just as it always had. Everything looked completely normal. Nothing out of place. And yet…for him, nothing would ever be the same again.

"Colt, it's been nearly two years, and you never said a word?"

He glanced over his shoulder at his twin. "Never could find a way to say it. Con, I still don't know what the hell happened." Shaking his head again, he huffed out a breath and tamped down the anger still rising within him. "I came home, got a divorce and figured it was done. No point in telling you about it when it was over."

"Can't believe you were *married*."

"You and me both," he muttered, and turned his gaze

back to the ocean, hoping for the calm that sight usually brought him. This time it didn't work. "I figured there was just nothing to tell."

"Yeah, well, you were wrong."

Understatement of the century.

"Looks that way." He had kids. Two of them. He could do the math, so he'd already worked out that they were eight months old. Eight months of their lives and he'd never even seen them. Never even guessed that they might exist. Cold fury rose up inside him again and he struggled to breathe past what felt like an iron band, tightening around his chest.

It had been close to two years since he'd seen Penny—though he'd thought about her far more often than he wanted to admit, even to himself. But at the moment, it wasn't memories driving him. Or the desire he'd once felt for her. It was cold fury, plain and simple. The kind of raw rage he'd never felt before. She'd kept his children from him and she'd done it deliberately. After all, it wasn't like he was hard to find. He was a King, for God's sake, and the Kings of California weren't exactly low profile.

"Fine. So what're you gonna do?"

Colt turned his back on the ocean and faced his twin. Steely determination fired his soul and filled his voice as he said, "I'm going to see my ex-wife. Then I'm going to get my kids."

Every time she moved, Penny felt a swift stab of pain. That didn't stop her from trying, though. Wincing, she shifted around carefully until she could reach the rolla-way table that held her laptop. Swinging it around, she then scooted up higher on the bed, moving much more slowly than she wanted to.

Penny was more accustomed to moving through life at top speed. She had a business and a home and two babies to care for, so hurrying was the only way she could keep up. Being forced to lie still in a hospital bed she couldn't afford was making her a little crazy.

Every moment she was stuck here was another dollar sign ticking up on the bill she would soon be handed. Every moment here, her babies were without her. And though Penny trusted her younger brother and his fiancée, Maria, completely, she missed the twins desperately. Since she worked out of her home, she was with them all the time. Being away from them made her feel as if she were missing a limb.

She reached out to pull the rolling table closer and gasped at the quick stab of pain slicing through her. "Ow!"

"You probably should lie still."

"Oh, God." Penny froze, hardly daring to breathe. She knew that voice. Heard it every night in her dreams. Clutching the edge of the table, only her eyes moved, tracking to the doorway where *he* stood. Colton King. The father of her children, the star of every one of her fantasies, her ex-husband and absolutely the last man on earth she wanted to see.

"Surprised?" he asked.

That word really didn't cover what she was feeling. "You could say that."

"Well then," he snapped, "you have some idea of how I feel."

Robert, she thought grimly. She was going to have to kill her little brother. Sure, she'd practically raised him and she loved him dearly. But for going to Colton and ratting her out, Robert had to pay. But dealing with her brother could come later. At the moment, she had to find a way to deal with her past.

"What're you doing here?"

He walked slowly into the room, his long legs crossing the linoleum-covered floor in a few easy strides. He moved almost lazily, but Penny wasn't fooled. She could feel the tension radiating off of him in thick waves and she braced herself for the confrontation that had been almost two years in the making.

His hands were tucked into the pockets of his black jeans. His thick-soled boots hardly made a whisper of sound as he moved. His black hair was a little too long, curling around the collar of his bloodred pullover shirt. But it was his eyes that held her. That mesmerized her as they had nearly two years ago.

They were the pale blue of an icy sky, fringed by lashes so thick and black any woman would have killed to have them. And right now, those cold eyes were fixed on her.

He was still the sexiest man she'd ever met. Still had that air about him that drew women to him like metal shavings to a magnet. Still made her want to throw both herself *and* a rock at him.

"Robert came to see me," he said lightly, as if it didn't mean a thing. But she knew better. Yes, they'd only been together for a week almost two years ago, but in those two years, Penny had relived every moment with him hundreds of times. At first, she had tried to forget him, because remembering only brought pain.

But then she'd found herself pregnant, and forgetting was impossible. So instead, she'd reveled in her memo-

ries. Kept them fresh and alive by mentally deconstruct-
ing every conversation, examining every moment spent
with him. She knew the tone of his voice. Knew the feel
of his skin, the taste of his lips.

And she knew, just by looking at him now, he was
angry.

Well then, they were a match. She didn't want him
here. Didn't *need* him here. Penny took a deep breath
and braced for the coming storm.

He stopped at the foot of her hospital bed and met her
gaze with a steely stare. "So," he said. "What's new?"

Anger flashed in those cool blue eyes and a muscle in
his jaw ticked spasmodically. One glance down to where
his hands were closed over the footboard showed that his
knuckles were white with the force of his grip.

"Robert had no right to go to you." Her fingers tugged
at the thin green blanket covering her.

Her brother had been after her since before the twins
were born to go to Colt and tell him the truth. But she'd
had her reasons for keeping her secret and nothing had
changed. Well, nothing but for the fact that her little
brother had turned traitor.

"Well," he said on a sharp, short laugh. "You're right
about *that,* anyway. *You* should have told me."

Ice coated his words as well as his eyes. No doubt he
was waiting for her to quiver and shrivel up beneath his
hard gaze. Well, Penny refused to back down or to feel
guilty about her decision. When she'd first discovered
she was pregnant, she'd gone around and around in her
mind, trying to figure out the best course of action.

She had argued with herself for weeks over what was
the right thing to do. Yes, she might have had an easier
time of it the last couple of years if she had gone to Colt

in the beginning. But she also might have spent the last two years tangled up in hard feelings, accusations and arguments. Not to mention a custody battle she wouldn't have stood a chance in. He was a *King,* for heaven's sake, and she didn't have enough money to buy lunch out!

So she'd chosen to keep the truth from him and she didn't regret it. How could she, when she knew she had done what she felt was in the best interests of her children?

With that thought firmly in mind, she got a grip on her own feelings as anger and frustration began to churn inside. "I understand how you feel but—"

"You understand *nothing.*" He cut her off as neatly as if he'd used a knife. "I just found out I'm a father. I have twins and I've never seen them." His white-knuckled grip on the foot rail of the bed tightened further and still his voice remained as cool and detached as the icy glare he had pinned on her. "I don't even know their *names.*"

She flushed. Fine. Yes. She could see how he felt. But that didn't mean what she'd done was wrong. Naturally, he wouldn't see it that way, but what Colton King thought of her really didn't matter, did it?

He never blinked. He only stared at her, with those ice-blue eyes narrowed as if he were focusing in an attempt to see into her mind and read all of her secrets. Thank heaven he couldn't.

"Their names, Penny. I've got a right to know the names of my children."

She hated this. Hated feeling as though she were setting her babies up to be let down by a father who didn't really want them. But she couldn't ignore his demand, either. Now that he knew about the twins, what was the point of trying to protect their anonymity?

"Okay. Your son's name is Reid and your daughter is Riley," she said.

He swallowed hard, took a deep breath and hissed it out again. "Reid and Riley *what?*"

She knew exactly what he meant. "Their last name is Oaks."

His mouth flattened into a grim line and it looked to Penny as if he were counting to ten. Slowly. "That'll change."

Panic shot through her, riding a lightning bolt of anger. "You think you can take over and change their names? No. You can't just walk back into my life and try to decide what's best for my children."

"Why the hell not?" he countered coldly. "You made that decision for *me* nearly two years ago."

"Colt—"

"Did you bother to list me as the father on their birth certificates?"

"Of course I did." Her twins had the right to know who their father was. And she would have told them… eventually.

"That's something at least," he muttered. "I'll have my lawyers take care of the legal name change."

"Excuse me?" She struggled to push herself upright and gasped as another sharp stab of pain hit in her abdomen. Breathless, she dropped back against her pillows.

He was at the side of the bed in an instant. "Are you all right? Do you need a nurse?"

"I'm fine," she lied tightly as the pain began to ebb into a just barely tolerable ache. "And no, I don't need a nurse." She needed pain medication. Privacy so she could cry. An eight-ounce glass of wine. "What I need is for you to leave."

"Not gonna happen," he told her.

She closed her eyes and muttered, "I could kill Robert for this."

"Yeah," Colt countered. "Someone finally being honest with me. There's a crime."

Her gaze snapped back to his. He was studying her as he would a bug under a microscope. Damn it, couldn't he have gotten fat in the last couple of years? Lost his hair? *Something?* Why did he still have to be the most gorgeous man she'd ever met? And wouldn't you just know that she'd have the conversation she had been dreading for nearly two years while trapped in a hospital bed? Wearing a god-awful gown? She was in pain, she was hungry because hospital food was appalling and God knew what her hair looked like.

Oh, that's good. Be worried about how you look, Penny.

Hard not to worry about it though, she told herself glumly. Especially when Colton King was standing right in front of her looking even better than he had two years ago. He'd taken her breath away the first time she'd seen him and apparently he had the same effect on her today.

"So when do you get out of here?" he asked, shattering her thoughts.

"Tomorrow probably." And she couldn't wait. Yes, she was in pain but she hated being in the hospital. She missed her babies. Plus, Penny didn't like having to ask Robert and Maria to watch her children. They had enough going on, with their wedding only a few weeks away.

In hindsight, she should have known that Robert would go to Colt. Should have guessed that her brother, thinking he was doing the right thing, would betray her secrets to the one man who should never have found out the truth. Oh, she was going to have plenty to say to her little brother once she was released from this antiseptic prison.

"Fine, then," Colt said flatly. "We'll continue this discussion once you're home."

Well, that caught her attention.

"No, we won't. This conversation is over, Colt."

"Not by a long shot." He stared down at her until Penny twitched uneasily, and then he warned, "You've got a hell of a lot of explaining to do."

"I don't owe you anything." But those words sounded hollow even to her.

She'd kept a huge secret from him and she'd done it deliberately. She knew that anyone standing on the outside of this relationship would call her some really descriptive names. But they wouldn't know *why* she'd done it. She hadn't even told Robert everything. Penny'd had reasons for her decisions and they were good ones. Ones she wouldn't regret, even while staring up into the cool blue eyes that still haunted her dreams.

He was angry and he had the right. But she'd had the right to do what she'd thought best for her children. And she wouldn't start second-guessing herself now.

"You're wrong about that," he told her softly, but the gentle tone of his voice did nothing to hide the fury crouched inside him.

A nurse bustled into the room, all business. "I'm sorry, you'll have to wait outside while I examine Ms. Oaks."

Penny's gaze never left Colt's and for a second or two, she thought he would argue, refuse to leave. Then he took a step back and nodded.

"Fine. I'll be back tomorrow to pick you up."

Panic shot through her. "Not necessary. Robert will pick me up."

The nurse was hovering and Penny could feel her gaze moving back and forth between the two of them.

"We don't need Robert's help. I'll be here in the morning."

"Oh," the nurse piped up, "she probably won't be released until early afternoon."

Colt paid no attention. "I'll be here tomorrow."

Then he stalked out of the room and didn't look back. Penny knew because she watched him go and continued to stare at the empty doorway long after the sound of his footsteps had faded.

"Wow," the nurse murmured. "Is that your husband?"

"No," Penny said. "He's—" What? A friend? An enemy? The father of her children? Her past come back to wreak havoc with her present? Since she couldn't say any of that, she said only, "He's my ex."

The nurse sighed. "Wow, can't believe you let that one get away."

It wasn't as if she'd had a choice. Still, to avoid more conversation, Penny closed her eyes and let the nurse get on with the examination.

But her mind wouldn't stop. Thoughts of Colt jammed up in her brain until all she could see were his eyes. Cold. Icy. Fixed.

And furious enough to make Penny wish tomorrow were years away.

Two

He didn't go to see his twins.

He wasn't up for that just yet.

Colt didn't want his children's first subconscious memory of their father to be of him furious.

So instead, he went to the beach. He needed to burn off some of the fury pumping through him. But the calm waves at Laguna weren't going to be enough to soothe the temper riding him. What he needed for that was blood-pumping action with a thread of danger. Enough to make his adrenaline high enough to swamp the anger chewing at him.

In Newport Beach, the Wedge was just at the end of the Balboa Peninsula and the waves there could reach thirty feet or more. Because of some "improvements" to the jetty in Newport Harbor sometime in the thirties, the waves here were highly unpredictable. One wave combined with another and then still another until the resulting wave was higher than anywhere else on the coast. Best part was, no two waves were alike, and where they would break was anybody's guess. Inexperienced surfers avoided the Wedge if they had any brains. As for Colt and the handful of other surfers out on this cold, autumn day...

The danger added to the fun.

Usually, anyway. Today, as he took wave after wave, riding the crest, being tossed into the sea and coming up in a froth of foam, his mind was too distracted to enjoy the rush. Images of Penny flashed through his mind on a continual loop. Visions of babies were there, too. Crying, laughing, sleeping. He couldn't clear his brain of the thoughts plaguing him, so he pushed himself harder, hoping for clarity. It didn't come though, and after a few hours in the punishing tempest of the sea, Colt had had enough. He dragged his board onto the sand and flopped down onto it.

Wrapping his arms around his knees, he stared out at the water and tried to make sense of what had happened that day. He'd never expected to see Penny Oaks again. Colt scrubbed one hand across his face and let himself remember her, lying in that hospital bed.

Through the anger, through the frustration and shock, he still had felt that jolt of sexual insanity he associated only with Penny. And *insanity* was the only word he could use to describe what she made him feel.

Penny, with her jeans and T-shirts and her lack of makeup or artifice of any kind, was just not the type of woman he was usually drawn to. He liked his women fast and sleek, with no expectations other than a great time in bed. Penny, though, was something else again. He'd known it instantly. But from that first moment at the convention nearly two years ago, he'd had to have her. One look at her and all he'd been able to think about was her long legs, wrapped around his waist. Her mouth pressed to his. Her breath warm against his skin.

And damned if she still didn't affect him that way.

Even lying in a hospital bed, with her long, dark red hair a tangle about her head, with her green eyes shining with both pain and panic, he'd wanted her so badly he'd had a hell of a time just walking out of the hospital.

After Vegas, he'd buried her memory and lost himself in dozens of temporary women. Yet he'd never really been able to wipe Penny from his mind entirely. And now she was back—with his *children*—and he'd be damned if he'd be cut out of his kids' lives. Even if, he was forced to admit, he was hardly father material.

The beach was nearly empty and the sunset stained the white clouds varying shades of pink and orange. The waves crashed relentlessly onto the shore, and out beyond the breakers, a few remaining surfers chased the next ride.

"You're an idiot."

Colt didn't have to turn around to know who had spoken. His twin's voice was unmistakable.

"Thanks for stopping by," he said. "Go away."

"Right. That'll happen." Instead, Connor settled down on the sand beside his brother and instinctively took up the same position as Colt. Arms wrapped around his drawn-up knees, gaze fixed on the ocean. They were so alike, they generally didn't even have to speak because each knew what the other was thinking.

But today, Colt realized, even *he* didn't know what he was thinking. Sexual desire, yes. Fury, oh, yes. But there was so much more. How the hell could he figure it out? Thoughts raced through his mind, slapped up against the wall of his brain and then rushed back down again to tangle with the others. Much like the legendary surf at the Wedge, Colt's mind at the moment was a dangerous place to be.

"You don't surf the Wedge alone and you know it," Connor said.

True. Even adrenaline junkies knew what line not to cross, but today, he just hadn't given a damn. Not that he would admit it to Connor.

"I wasn't alone," Colt argued. "There are at least a dozen other guys out there."

"Yeah, all looking out for themselves. Don't suppose you noticed the riptide?"

"I noticed," he admitted grudgingly. Riptides were a danger on their own. Riptides at the Wedge were a whole new level of risky. Get caught in one of those and you could be dragged out to sea so far you wouldn't have the strength to swim back in. "And I don't need you nagging me."

"Fine. Won't nag. Just leave a note behind next time you surf here alone, okay?"

"A note?" He looked at his twin.

Connor shrugged. "You're gonna commit suicide the least you can do is leave a note—you could say, 'I should have listened to Connor.'"

Colt shook his head and returned his gaze to the churning sea. White water and spray shot into the air. A cold sea wind whipped his hair back from his forehead, and overhead, gulls shrieked like the dying.

He didn't even wonder how Connor had known to find him here. For the last ten years, Colt had spent most of his time chasing the next adventure. Always searching out danger and beating it. He just wasn't the office, suit-and-tie kind of guy.

Hell, even with floor-to-ceiling windows displaying a spectacular view of the Pacific Ocean and the California coastline, he felt trapped in the building he and Connor owned on the Pacific Coast Highway. Which was why, he reminded himself, *he* was the adventure man and his twin was in charge of paperwork.

He shuddered at the thought of being buried behind a desk. Like the clients that King's Extreme Adventures served, Colt was always looking for the next shot of adrenaline. Skydiving, BASE jumping, extreme surfing, wingsuit flying—he'd done them all and had no intention of ever stopping.

In spite of what he'd learned today.

"Have you seen the twins?"

"No." Colt narrowed his gaze on the ocean and tried to ignore the sudden, frantic beat of his heart.

"Why not?"

"Because I'm too pissed at their mother."

Connor laughed shortly. "I'm guessing their mom's not real fond of you about now, either."

He turned his head to glare at his brother. "You think that matters to me?"

"No. But I know the kids do."

Well, that took the fire out of him. "What the hell do I know about being a father?"

Connor shrugged. "We had a pretty good role model for that, I think."

"Yeah, we did." Their parents had been the best. Until... Guilt reared up inside him, shouting to be heard, but he shut it down as he always did. The past didn't have any meaning here. This was all about the now. And the future. "Doesn't mean I'll be any good at it."

"Doesn't mean you'll suck, either."

Colt laughed and pushed one hand through his still-wet hair. "Quite the pep talk."

Connor grinned and turned his gaze on the ocean. "You don't need a pep talk. Unless you don't believe they're your kids..."

"No." Colt shook his head and scowled. Naturally, he'd considered that for a split second, right after Robert Oaks had punched him. But he'd discounted it just as quickly. "One thing Penny is not is a liar. In spite of the fact that she hid them from me. Besides," he reasoned, "if she was trying to push someone else's twins off as mine, she'd have come to me for money right from the jump."

"True. Still, you should do a paternity test. Cover all your bases legally."

He would, eventually. Colt wasn't an idiot. But tests or no tests, he knew, in his gut, those twins were his. Penny had been too panicked about him finding out about them to have him doubting it for a second. And she was right to panic, he told himself. Because things were going to change. Her life as she knew it was now over.

Because Colton King would do whatever he had to to make sure his kids were taken care of.

* * *

Maybe he'd forgotten to come.

Penny laughed silently at the very idea. Colton King might look like a wild, untamed, crazy adventurer—and he was. But he was also a brilliant businessman who never forgot a detail.

So then if he hadn't forgotten, why hadn't he shown up at the hospital this morning as promised? Penny had spent a long, sleepless night, worrying about what she would say to him when he strolled into her room again. Turned out, she needn't have bothered.

All day, she'd been tied in knots, waiting for him to appear. And he never showed up. Why that should irritate her when she really wished he would just go away and stay away, she didn't know.

But then, her feelings for Colton King had always confused her. That one week with him had fueled her dreams and her fantasies for months. Even when she was pregnant with the twins he had known nothing about, her mind continued to plague her every night, with alternative endings to their time together. But every morning, she was dragged back to a reality where happily ever afters didn't exist.

"And you should remember that," she muttered, giving herself a warning. Yet even while that thought squirmed through her mind, her body bristled with nervous expectation and she couldn't quite seem to calm it down.

Penny had spent most of the day—when she wasn't torturing herself with thoughts of Colt—trying desperately to be released from the hospital. Not only couldn't she afford a lengthy stay—they probably charged a hundred dollars for an aspirin—but she needed to get home.

To be with her kids. To be back at her cottage, tucked away from everything so she could… What? *Hide?* From Colt? Not a chance. Now that he knew the twins existed, Penny would never be free of him.

Her heart rate suddenly jumped into overdrive and she groaned. For heaven's sake, would she *always* have that reaction to the man? Wasn't being tossed aside once enough of a lesson? Did she really want to let him back into her life so he could do it again?

"No way," she vowed and tossed an angry glance at the still-empty doorway.

A half an hour ago, her stupid doctor had finally arrived to give her one more check and sign her release papers. But had a nurse shown up to wheel her out? No. And every second that passed increased the chances of Colt at last deciding to make an appearance.

Which made her wonder again why he hadn't come. What was he off doing? Was he at her house, insinuating himself with two babies who wouldn't have the slightest idea how to protect their hearts? Or maybe, she thought wistfully, he'd changed his mind? Decided to ignore his children after all? Could she be that lucky?

Not a chance, and she knew it. One thing she was sure of as far as the Kings of California were concerned: family meant everything.

During their brief time together, how many stories had Colt told her about his brothers, his cousins, their wives and kids? He'd painted amazing pictures of family gatherings and weddings and christenings, and she'd been both jealous of their deep family connection and intimidated by it.

She didn't know anything about big families. All she'd

had in the world was her younger brother and for years it had been the two of them—united against all comers. Heck, she hadn't even had a social life before she'd met Colton King and tossed her heart at his feet. She hadn't exactly been a virgin, but the two encounters before Colt had left her convinced that every woman on the face of the planet was lying about the whole earth-shattering-stars-exploding-orgasm thing.

Which might explain why she'd fallen so hard and so fast for Colt. She actually had seen stars with him. She'd felt things with him she wouldn't have believed herself capable of. He'd made her feel beautiful and sexy and desirable. He'd swept her off her feet so completely, she'd obviously managed to confuse lust with love. Just look where that had gotten her.

A marriage that hadn't even been twenty-four hours old when it was dissolved.

She turned her head and looked out the window to a patch of blue sky just visible beyond an old elm tree. Leaves dipped and swayed in the wind she wished she could feel on her face. Maybe it would help clear away all the clutter in her mind.

Because now all she could think of was that last morning with Colt. The day she'd awakened as a bride and in less than ten minutes had become yesterday's news.

For the past week, they'd spent every possible moment in bed, wrapped up in each other, shutting the rest of the world out of the bubble of passion they'd created. Then on the last night of the convention, they'd been married and had spent hours making love, unable to keep their hands off each other.

But the following morning, with the first feeble rays

of sunrise creeping over the sky, Penny had opened her eyes to find Colt standing beside the bed. He was dressed and packed and the expression on his face was grim. Her heart sank and then shattered when he spoke.

"I'm not the marrying kind, Penny." He pushed one hand through his hair, huffed out an exasperated breath and continued. "Last night was…a mistake. I don't want a wife. I don't want kids. Picket fences and the family dog give me hives. This week was nice and the sex was great, but that's all we share."

When she tried to speak, he cut her off with a negligent wave of his hand. "I'll have my lawyer take care of the divorce."

Finally, one word slipped past the tight knot in her throat. "Divorce?"

"It's best. For both of us." He slung his duffel bag over his shoulder, gave her one last look and said, "I'll have the papers sent to you. Goodbye, Penny."

And he was gone.

As if their incredible week together had never happened. As if he hadn't spent every waking moment learning every square inch of her body. As if it was all… nothing.

She could hardly be expected to have warm, fuzzy feelings for him after that, right? And the hot, undulating need she felt was *not* the same thing at all.

"Oh, this is so not good."

"Ready to go?" A nurse she'd never seen before popped into the room pushing an empty wheelchair and Penny should have been delighted. But her short trip down memory lane had sort of put a damper on her emotions. Now the time was here. She was leaving the expensive-but-slightly-safer atmosphere of the hospital for her home, where Colton would be showing up, and there was no time left to hide. Nowhere she could run.

But as that thought rose up in her mind, she remembered that scene in the Vegas hotel room again and instinctively stiffened her shoulders. Why should *she* run? She'd done nothing wrong. She'd only protected her kids from the same heartache she had experienced. She wouldn't stand by and see their little hearts break when their daddy walked away from them without a backward glance.

"Yes," she said, lifting her chin, already preparing for the battle she knew was coming. "I'm ready."

Or as ready as she would ever be.

The efficient nurse pushed her down the hall to the elevator and from there down a long hall headed for the lobby and the wide front doors. As they passed the billing office, Penny turned her head to look up at the nurse. "I'm sorry, but I still have to make financial arrangements and—"

"Oh, sweetie, that's been taken care of."

"What?"

The nurse smiled down at her, clearly not registering the look of shock carved into Penny's features.

"Your husband took care of all of that this morning. He didn't want you to worry about a thing. Gotta say, you picked a good one there."

"A good one—my husband—" Dread coiled in the pit of her stomach and sent spindly threads swimming through her veins. Colt had paid her hospital bill. Colt had walked in and taken over and everyone at the hospital had simply fallen into line.

Why that should surprise her she didn't know. He had the ability to make people jump whether they wanted to or not. Colton King expected to get his own way and knew just how to maneuver people into giving it to him. He'd probably never once considered that she might not want his help. He'd simply done as he always did—steamroller over everything in his path to get what he wanted.

She fumed silently in her wheelchair. It wouldn't do the slightest bit of good to argue with the hospital. Of course they'd appreciate her bill being paid in full rather than the monthly payments she was going to arrange. Why wouldn't they take a lump sum? It wasn't as if *they* were going to be indebted to the man. But for Penny, this was just one more link to Colt. A link she didn't want. She hadn't *asked* him to ride to the rescue, had she? No. And now, if she wanted to hang on to her pride, she'd have to find a way to pay him back.

The nurse wheeled her outside and the first breath of fresh, salt air lightened Penny's mood dramatically. Until she saw him.

Colt lounged against a black luxury SUV, his arms folded over his chest, his long legs crossed at the ankle. He looked relaxed, casual, in his boots, blue jeans and dark red shirt. He wore dark glasses over his ice-blue eyes and the wind ruffled his black hair. She thought she heard the nurse behind her give a soft sigh of pure female appreciation, and Penny completely understood.

Just looking at the man was enough to send most women into orgasmic shock. And she was in a better position than most to know that no matter how good a fantasy a woman could spin around him, reality with Colt was so much better.

And in spite of her churning thoughts and suddenly heated, throbbing body, her first instinct was to ask the nurse to turn around. To take her back inside. To run and hide, she was ashamed to admit, even to herself. So she swallowed her nerves, plastered a fake smile on her face and prepared to give the performance of a lifetime.

"Here she is, all ready to go home," the nurse cooed as Colt pushed off the car and walked closer.

"Right. Thanks." He slipped one hand under Penny's arm and helped her stand. Since her knees were feeling a little weak at the moment, she was grateful for the assistance. Even though it was *his* fault her knees were weak in the first place.

"You okay?" he asked, his voice a husky whisper close to her ear.

She closed her eyes and held her breath. If she had one whiff of his scent, it might just finish her off. "I'm fine. Thanks for picking me up."

He smirked as if he knew she hadn't meant a word of that and Penny ground her teeth together. The man was irritating on so many levels. Not the least of which was his apparent ability to read her mind.

She busied herself with the seat belt, only wincing once or twice as she settled herself into the wide, extremely comfortable leather seats. An unwanted comparison to her worn-out four-door sedan jumped into her mind, but she pushed it away again. Her car might not be shiny, with leather seats—and ooh, a minitelevision in the dashboard—but it got her where she was going. So far.

Colt climbed into the driver's seat, tossed her bag of

personal items into the back, then fired up the engine. He hooked his seat belt, checked the mirrors—in fact, did everything but look directly at her. Finally, Penny couldn't stand it.

"Why are you here?"

He glanced at her briefly. "To take you home."

"Robert was supposed to pick me up."

"We came to a different arrangement."

"You *have* to stop interfering in my life."

"No, I really don't."

He steered the car down the driveway and out into traffic and she was quiet as the familiar landscape flashed past. Buildings and cars on the left, the ocean on the right as he drove down the Pacific Coast Highway. Sunlight glinted on the surface of the water and made her eyes sting. That's why they felt teary. Not because of the helpless sensation beginning to build inside her.

"You're quiet," he observed. "Unusual for you as I remember."

"People change."

"Not normally," he said. "People are who they are. But situations…*they* change."

And here we go, she thought.

"You should have told me," he said tightly and she risked a quick look at him. His profile was rugged, breathtakingly gorgeous and hard as stone.

"You didn't want to know," she said.

"I don't remember being given a choice."

"Funny," she muttered, as the memory of their last morning together rose up in her mind again, "I remember."

"I don't know what the hell you're talking about."

How could he have forgotten? He'd made his choice long before they even met. But that last morning with him, he'd shared it all with her, searing the memories into her mind. If she closed her eyes, she could still see his face, hear his voice and then finally, the receding sound of his footsteps as he walked out of her life.

"I want to know everything, Penny." He stopped for a red light and threw her a hard look. "Every damn thing that's happened over the last two years."

"Eighteen months."

"Sue me," he snapped. "I rounded up."

The light turned green and he stepped on the gas. With his gaze locked on the road, he said, "And when that conversation begins, you can start by telling me *why* you thought it was a good idea to hide my kids from me."

"We're not in hiding."

"You know what I mean."

Yeah, she did. And that's exactly what she had done, though it sounded a lot colder when he said it out loud. "I had my reasons."

"Can't wait to hear them," he assured her.

Outside the car, it was a typical fall day in Southern California. Sun shining, clear sky, about sixty-five degrees. Inside the car, however, it was midwinter in the Arctic. Penny wouldn't have been surprised to see ice forming on the dashboard. Colt burned cold when he was furious. She'd seen it firsthand at the convention when they'd met.

Their third day together, Penny was running her booth, trying to win some clients for her fledgling sports photography business. A drunk stumbled onto the convention floor from the casino and had made Penny miserable. Hanging about her booth, demanding a kiss she had no intention of giving him. Chasing away potential clients.

But she'd been handling him until he made a grab for her—and before she could take care of the situation herself, Colton had been there. Icy rage in his eyes, he'd grabbed the drunk by the collar of his shirt and half dragged, half walked him off the floor. When he came back to her, Colt's anger was gone, but concern had been flashing in his eyes and Penny could remember feeling... cherished. Say what you would about equality, it was hard *not* to feel a thrill when a man was so protective.

He'd come to her rescue and then treated her as if she were made of glass instead of treating her like the fiercely independent woman she was. And she'd loved every minute of it.

He was excitement and tenderness and sex all rolled into one. No wonder she'd fallen so hard, she told herself. No woman in the world would have been able to resist Colton King. That week with him had been the most magical of her life. In a few short days, she'd fallen so completely in love with him. She'd even married him in a sweet, shabby chapel and told herself that it was meant to be. She'd indulged in dreams and imaginings and let herself drift on a tide of the most incredible sex she'd ever experienced and thought somehow that it would all work out.

Until, of course, the world came crashing down on her and reality took a bite of her heart.

And now cold, hard reality was back to do it all again. But this time, she wouldn't let herself be vulnerable to him. This time, she wouldn't make the mistake of thinking that a man who showed such passion in bed *must* feel something for her. This time, she was ready for Colton King.

"You were never going to tell me, were you?"

"No," she said, not even bothering to give him her list of reasons. They wouldn't make a difference to him. He didn't care *why*—only that she hadn't told him.

"Well, I know now."

"It doesn't change anything, Colt," she said, turning her head to look at his gorgeous, unyielding profile.

Heat stirred inside her, despite the lingering pain of her emergency surgery. Despite the fact that she hadn't seen him in eighteen months. Even despite the fact that the morning after their spur-of-the-moment marriage, he'd walked out on her, promising that a divorce lawyer would be in contact with her.

The only reason he was back now was because of the twins. Her babies. And he wasn't going to get them. She lifted one hand to rub her forehead in a futile attempt to ease the headache making her eyes throb.

"It changes everything and you know it," he said, voice as tight as the grip he had on the steering wheel. "You should have told me. You had no right to keep my children from me."

"Rights?" Stunned, headache forgotten, she stared at him as the humiliation of the last time she'd seen him washed over her. "I absolutely had the right to do whatever I had to do to protect my kids."

"From their *father?*"

"From anyone who might hurt them."

His features went stone-still but his eyes were flashing. "And you think I'd hurt them?"

"Not physically, of course not," she snapped. "But you walked away from me, remember? You're the one who said you didn't want to hear from me again. You're the one who told me that the week we spent together was 'fun' but over. Not to mention when you added that the thought of kids gave you hives. Any of this ringing a bell?"

"All of it," he said. "But I didn't know you were pregnant, did I?"

"Neither did I."

"Yeah, but you knew soon after and you didn't *tell* me."

"It wasn't any of your business."

He laughed but there was no humor in the sound. "Not my business. I have two children and they're none of my business."

"I have two kids. *You* have nothing."

"If that's what you really think, you're in for a surprise."

He made the turn that would take him to her house and Penny frowned. "How do you know where I live?"

"Amazing what you can find out if you're motivated." He glanced at her, then shifted his gaze back to the shady, tree-lined street in front of him. "For example. I know your business is getting a slow start—switched from sports photography to babies—an interesting choice. I know you don't have health insurance. And I know that you're living in your grandmother's cottage in Laguna." He took a breath and continued. "Your brother's engaged to Maria Estrada and is a general practice intern at Huntington Beach hospital. You're living off your credit cards and your car is fifteen years old." He spared her another look. "Did I miss anything?"

No, he hadn't. In fact, Penny worried about what else

he might have found out. He'd scratched the surface of her life, but just how deeply had he continued to dig?

"What gives you the right to pry, Colt?" She didn't like the idea of her past being spread out for him to pick over. Didn't like feeling as though she'd been exposed. "We spent one week together nearly two years ago."

"And apparently," he added, "we made two babies." He pulled up in front of her house and parked. When he turned the engine off, he faced her and his eyes looked like chips of ice. "That gives me any right I want to claim."

To avoid looking at him, she stared at the house she loved. A tiny Tudor with dark shutters and beams flat against cream-colored stucco and leaded windows that winked in the last lights of the sun. Ivy climbed along the porch railings and chrysanthemums bloomed dark yellow and purple in the front flower bed. The house was small and cozy and had always, even when she was a child, signified safety and warmth to Penny.

Now she looked at it and felt a sense of peace she desperately needed steal over her.

"I'm not going anywhere, Penny. Get used to it."

Peace dissolved as a stir of heat erupted inside her again and Penny wanted to shriek with frustration. *How* could her body respond to a man her brain realized was nothing but trouble? She felt as if she'd been stripped bare in front of him. Her life was nothing more than a series of facts that he felt free to dissect in a cold, dispassionate speech.

But then, that was Colton's way, wasn't it? she reminded herself. Unemotional. Detached.

Distanced from any sort of real human contact, he

kept his heart—if he had one—locked away behind a steel door that was, as far as she could tell, impenetrable.

Her voice was barely a whisper when she looked into his eyes and asked, "What exactly do you want, Colt?"

"That's easy," he said with a shrug. "I want what's *mine*."

A cold, tight fist closed around her heart as he got out of the car, slammed the door and walked around to her side. His? She knew he didn't mean that he wanted *her,* so he was talking about her kids. Her *babies*. Fear coiled around her heart and made breathing almost impossible. But where she might try to run and hide to protect herself—to safeguard her children she was willing to walk into hell itself.

She watched him through the car window and when he opened her door to help her out, she looked into his eyes and said, "You can't have them."

Three

"You can't have my kids, Colt." Her voice hitched higher. "I won't let you."

"You can't stop me," he told her flatly.

Colton had done a lot of thinking in the last twenty-four hours and he'd come to one conclusion. If these were his children, then he wouldn't be shut out. And frankly, even though he'd already arranged for a paternity test, he knew, deep in his gut, there wasn't a need for one. When he and Penny were together, she'd been with only two other men before him. She was honest. Straightforward. So deeply moral that she'd never try to pass off another man's child as his. Hell, her sweet-natured decency was one of the reasons he'd run from her so fast.

Colt wasn't interested in being with a woman who had romance in her eyes and a plan for the future in her heart. Normally, he didn't *do* a "future." He did "now."

And normally, he preferred women who wanted nothing more than he did out of a temporary relationship. Good sex, a few laughs and an easy exit.

There was *nothing* easy about Penny Oaks.

Colton watched a flash of fire in her eyes and knew she wouldn't surrender without a fight. On any other day, he might have admired it. But not today. Today, he was the one with the claim on fury. He was the one who'd been kept in the dark for nearly two years. No, he didn't want to be married. He'd never planned on being a father—his life was too risky for that—but now that he *was* a father, things had changed.

And, he told himself grimly, they were going to change even more, soon.

"You don't want the twins," she said softly, her gaze locked with his. "You only want to hurt me."

Hurt her? What he wanted to do at the moment was kiss her until neither of them could breathe. He wanted to reach into the car, drag her out and plaster her up against him so that he could feel every one of the curves he remembered so well. Even through the anger, through the frustration and confusion, desire was clear and simple. Unfortunately, nothing else about this situation was.

"I'm not interested in hurting you." Understatement. "But I do want answers." He planted one hand on the roof of the car and leaned in closer to her. "And you don't want to challenge me, Penny. I always find a way to win."

"Win?" Her mouth dropped open. "This isn't a game, Colt. This is about two babies."

"*My* babies," he corrected, and felt a hitch in his chest as he said those words. Since yesterday, he'd done little else but think about the bombshell that had been dropped into the middle of his world. Everything around him felt as if it were slightly off balance. As if the steady, familiar course of his life had been suddenly turned into a roller coaster ride, with dips and turns hidden around every corner.

There were two kids who deserved a father. It was just their bad luck to have gotten *him* in the genetic lottery. He couldn't give them stability. A man to count on. Everything he'd had growing up. Still, he'd do the best he could by them because he owed them that.

"What're you doing, Colt?" She stared up at him, wariness and pain shining in her eyes.

"What needs to be done," he ground out, refusing to be swayed by the naked emotion he saw on her face.

What he had to remember was that she'd kept his children from him. So much for the "honesty" he'd seen in her at the beginning, he thought cynically. Hell, maybe she was really no different from the countless other women who had tried to convince a King that she was pregnant just to be able to dip into his bank account.

But she was different, wasn't she? She'd made no effort to contact him. Hadn't asked for money. Hadn't gone to a tabloid, selling her story to make some fast cash. Hell, she'd gone out of her way to avoid telling him about the twins. Hadn't once considered him in any of the decisions she'd made in the last couple of years.

Well, all of that was going to change. She might not be interested in cashing in on the King name. Might have no desire at all for him to be a part of her world. But she was about to find out just what it was like having a King in the family picture.

"We have to talk," he ground out, keeping his voice low and his gaze locked on hers. "The question is, do you

want to do it now, with your brother watching us from
your front window—"

She shifted a look to the house at his words and huffed
out a breath. Colt had noticed Robert the instant he'd
parked in front of the cottage. The man looked just as
constipated and irritated as he had the day before. But
at least now, Colt could understand why he was such a
pain in the ass.

"Or do you want to go inside, get rid of the audience
and do this in private? Your choice."

A couple of tense seconds ticked past.

"Fine," she grumbled, unhooking her seat belt and
wincing a bit as she tried to get out of the car. "But this
isn't over."

"That's the first thing you've gotten right," he promised, feeling a twinge of sympathy mixed with concern
when he watched her trying to move through pain that
was clearly bothering her more than she wanted to admit.
Irritated at her stubborn independence even in the face
of real discomfort, he reached into the car and lifted her
out. He should have put her down at once, of course,
but he noticed that her face was so pale that the freckles across her nose and cheeks shone like flakes of gold
against snow.

"You can set me down now," she said, tipping her face
back to look up at him.

But he didn't want to. He liked holding her. Hell, it
was feeding that need to touch her. She felt…right, cra-
dled against his chest, and that weird thought worried
him quite a bit. But at least *lust* he knew how to deal with.

"I'm perfectly capable of walking."

"Sure you are." He shook his head as he looked down
at her. His body tightened further and it was his turn to

camouflage a wince of pain. "And it'll take you twenty minutes to get to the front door. This is faster."

She glowered at him, but Colt paid no attention. Hard to focus on her irritation when every inch of his body was reacting to her closeness. Holding her to him stirred up feelings he'd just as soon leave buried. But it was too late. Her T-shirt and jeans were worn and soft. Her curves fit nicely against him and with every breath she took, she fired the heat already scorching him.

"Just hold still, will you?" Still shaking his head, not sure if he was angrier with her or with his own reaction, Colt took the crooked, flower-lined sidewalk up to the steps. Robert opened the door and Colt carried her across the porch and into the house.

His first impression was that the place had been built for really short people. It was like a dollhouse. Cute to look at but impossible to move around in. He had to duck his head to avoid a low-hanging beam separating the entry from the postage-stamp-sized living room. And suddenly he felt like Gulliver. All that was missing were the ropes tying him down—although there were two tiny ropes somewhere in this house, prepared to do the job.

"You okay, Penny?" Robert asked as Colt deposited her gently on the overstuffed couch.

"She's fine," Colt answered for her. "I almost never beat a woman."

Robert sneered. "Is that supposed to be funny?"

"Not really," Colton told him. "Nothing about this situation is funny."

"I'm fine," Penny said, shooting Colt a look that plainly said *I can speak for myself.* Then she turned back to her brother. "How are the twins?"

Robert threw a look over his shoulder at the hallway

behind him. "Sleeping. We took them for a long walk and the fresh air just knocked 'em out. Maria's checking on them."

"Good," she said, a smile curving her mouth. "Thanks so much for watching the babies. I can't wait to see them."

"Me, either." Colt looked from Penny to Robert and back again and had the satisfaction of seeing her squirm uncomfortably.

"For what it's worth," Robert told him, "I've been after her from the beginning to tell you about the twins."

"Too bad you weren't more successful."

"She's too stubborn for her own good," her brother argued. "Once she makes up her mind, you couldn't blow her off course with dynamite." He glanced at his sister. "And it's not like I enjoyed going behind her back to tell you the truth. I'm just tired of seeing her struggle when she shouldn't have to."

"I understand. And I remember just how stubborn she is." In fact, Colt recalled plenty about the week he and Penny had spent together what felt like a lifetime ago. He remembered her laughter. He remembered the feel of her curled against him in the middle of the night. The taste of her mouth, the scent of her skin. And he remembered seeing rainbows and promises shining in her green eyes.

It had spooked him, plain and simple. No other woman before her or since had ever gotten so close to him. No other woman had ever made him so drugged on passion that he'd proposed and married her before he could come to his senses.

And no other woman's memory had stayed with him as hers had.

God knows he'd tried to bury her memory, but it just wouldn't stay gone. He could be halfway around the world, exploring some new adventure, and hear a soft, feminine laugh—and just for a second, he'd turn and search the crowd for her familiar face. He had dreams that were so clear, so *real,* that he would wake up expecting to find her lying next to him.

She'd done that to him. One week with Penny had threatened everything in his life. Of course he'd had to leave her.

"Since you remember, you know what it's like trying to argue with her," Robert was saying.

"Oh, I don't intend to argue." Colt glanced at Penny and watched as sparks glinted in her eyes. "I'm just going to tell her how things are going to be."

"That I'd like to see," Robert murmured.

"Maybe I'll sell tickets."

"If you two are quite finished," Penny announced.

"Not even close," Colt told her.

"Not my problem anymore," Robert said, lifting both hands in gratitude at being able to hand off the responsibility of worrying about his sister. He looked at Colt. "Good luck."

"Not necessary." Colt didn't need luck. All he needed was a cold shower and then a chance to settle a few things with the mother of his children.

"Seriously?" Penny tried to get up off the couch, but Colt dropped one hand onto her shoulder to hold her in place.

"Don't move from that spot."

"You are not in charge here," she argued.

"Wanna bet?"

He met her gaze and stared, waiting for her to back off first. In a contest of wills, Penny wouldn't stand a chance. She could be as stubborn as she liked, but she hadn't been raised a King. In the King family, *everyone* wanted to be right. And no one ever backed down. So if she thought she could best him in a staring contest, she couldn't be more wrong.

Took a few seconds, but eventually, she shifted her gaze from his and slumped back into the floral cushions, muttering a steady stream of words he was probably better off not hearing. A reluctant smile twitched his lips. He had to admire her fighting spirit—even though she had no hope of winning.

A pretty, dark-haired woman with big brown eyes walked into the room, passed Robert and Colt, then took a seat on the coffee table in front of Penny. Reaching out, she took Penny's hands in hers and squeezed. "The twins are fine. They're sound asleep and since it was so late in the afternoon, we fed them their dinner, too. I know it's a little early, but with any luck, they'll sleep the night through and give you some rest."

"Thanks, Maria. I really appreciate you stepping in to help."

"We both appreciate it," Colton said.

Finally, the woman lifted her gaze to his and there was no warmth in her eyes. She looked him up and down and Colt had the distinct impression she was less than impressed. He almost smiled again. He admired loyalty, too.

"Of course we helped," she said coolly. "Penny had *no one* else."

"Maria…" Robert gave a sigh.

Colt shook his head and waved one hand, dismissing Robert's objection. Now he knew two new things about Penny. Her little brother was willing to use his fists to defend her, and her friend Maria was Penny's staunch ally.

Still, all three of them had better get used to how things were going to be. "Now she does have someone else."

"We'll see, won't we?" Maria turned her gaze back to Penny and said, "If you need anything, just call. Honestly, I can be over in minutes."

Penny laughed a little. "I will. Promise."

"Good." Nodding abruptly, Maria leaned forward, kissed Penny's cheek and said, "We'll go now. I'm sure you two have plenty to talk about."

"Oh, you don't have to leave so soon."

"Yeah, they do," Colt argued, and Penny shot him a hard glare. Didn't bode well for their "discussion" but that wouldn't have gone well in any case, he assured himself.

"Okay then," Robert announced and took Maria's hand in his, drawing her up from her perch on the edge of the table. "Remember, if you need something, call."

Then it was just the two of them. Colton didn't even know where to begin. There was a lot he wanted to know and even more he *needed* to know—things like why bother buying and using condoms if they clearly didn't work? An existential question he'd have to explore more completely later. There were plenty of other things he wanted to know, though.

But at the moment, damned if he could think of a thing to say. Instead, he stared down at the woman he'd married and divorced within the span of a week and tried not to notice just how blasted vulnerable she looked. Hard to have the kind of argument that was waiting for them when the woman was just out of the hospital.

Hospital.

That word conjured up old mental images that threatened to choke him. He had promised to be there in Pen-

ny's room that morning, but hadn't been able to do it.
Couldn't force himself to walk back into that building.
Into a place so filled with the scent of fear and misery,
so thick with memories that Colt felt them surrounding
him, burying him. Even now, his mind was opening the
door to the darkness that hid deep within his past. Shadows rushed out and spilled through his body like black
paint, covering everything in its path.

Shaken right down to the bone, Colt reached out
blindly and grabbed hold of the anger that was his sal-
vation. If he could just focus on the situation facing him
now and shut down the past, he'd get through this. As
he'd done so many times before.

"Are you okay?"

"What?" He surfaced from the tangled thoughts in his
mind like a surfer trying to breathe through sea foam.
"What? Oh. Yeah. I'm fine."

She didn't look convinced, but that didn't bother him.
The real problem here was that he was still drawn to her.
Still felt that nearly magnetic pull that he'd felt so long
ago. What was it about her, he asked himself, that tugged
at everything inside him? And why the hell couldn't he
get rid of it?

Trying to avoid looking at Penny, he glanced around
the small beach cottage and really noticed it for the first
time.

The rooms were small and painted a soft yellow that
looked as though sunbeams lived in the walls. An old,
stone-faced fireplace stood along one side of the room,
with built-in bookcases on either side.

A painting of the sea hung on the wall above the hearth,
and around the room, old but comfortable-looking furniture sprawled, inviting people to come in and take it easy.

Reading lamps sat on the end tables and there was a huge plastic tub filled with toys beneath the front window.

Off the living room was a hall that probably led to the bedrooms and a dining room with a door beyond that was undoubtedly hiding the kitchen. It was a typical cottage, no doubt built in the forties for long weekends at the beach. The rooms were small, the yard tiny and if you had claustrophobia you wouldn't last out the weekend. But there were charms in these old neighborhoods, too. Close to the beach, on a quiet night, you could hear the surf. Decades-old trees lined the streets and their roots caused sidewalks to ripple like waves. And any time the city tried to pull down the trees to make the sidewalks even, the neighborhoods came out in full fight mode.

Places like this never changed.

"You hungry?" he asked suddenly, to break the silence.

"I'll make something in a minute," she said and eased back into the cushions of the couch.

"I'll make it." When she looked at him in surprise, he almost laughed. He'd been on his own for a long time and though he had a housekeeper, he'd never bothered to hire a cook. Hell, he wasn't home often enough to justify it. "I'm not completely helpless in the kitchen."

"That's not what you said—" Her voice trailed away.

"What?"

She shook her head and stared up at the ceiling. Old, smoke-stained beams divided the cream-colored plaster. "That week we were together, you told me that you and your twin once set fire to your aunt's kitchen when you were trying to make French toast."

He frowned to himself. He didn't remember telling her that, and knowing that he obviously *had* told her confused the hell out of him. Colt didn't usually share much of himself with women—hell, with anyone. He didn't want the closeness and didn't crave what women always seemed to enjoy—the baring of souls. Who the hell wanted a naked soul?

He gave her a tight smile. "Been a long time since the fire in the kitchen. I'm not bad with chicken or pasta, though I'm the first to admit I'm not a chef. But I make great phone calls for takeout."

She laughed a little, then winced, and Colt felt a twinge in response. But when she spoke, all sympathy for her drained away.

"Look, Colt, I know we have to talk but I'm just too tired to deal with you tonight." She sighed a little. "Why don't you go home and we'll talk in a day or two?"

"Go home?" He repeated it because he couldn't believe she would even suggest it. He was here now and he wasn't leaving. Not yet, anyway. "And who takes care of the twins while you sit here on the couch and chew at your lip?"

She stopped that instantly and fired a look at him. "I can manage. I always do."

"No," he corrected. "You always *have* in the past. Now that's not an option."

"You're not in charge here, Colt."

"Check again." He walked closer to her and gave her a glare designed to intimidate. From what he could tell, it didn't work. "Damn it, Penny, as mad as I am at you right now, I'd almost be willing to do just what you said and leave you here on your own just so you could see what a stupid decision that would be—"

"Bye then."

"I said *almost*." Sinking to his heels beside the couch,

he met her eyes and said, "As much as you hate the idea, you need me. Damn it, I had to carry you into the house."

"I could have walked."

"What is bothering you the most?" he asked. "Needing help? Or needing *me?*"

"You're wrong, Colt," she said. "I don't need you. Okay, maybe I need some help, but I don't need *you.*"

"Tough." He straightened up again, looming over her and forcing her to keep her head tipped back just to meet his eyes.

"'Cause you've got me. Until we get this whole mess straightened out, I'm not going anywhere."

She huffed out an impatient breath. "Don't you have a mountain to climb? A building to jump off of?"

For one split second, thoughts of Mount Etna and his Sicilian trip floated through his mind. Then he let it go. "There's plenty of time for that. Right now, you're the only adventure in my future."

"Swell." She leaned forward, braced one hand on the arm of the couch and hissed in a breath.

"What're you doing?"

She flashed him a look of pure irritation. "I'm going to check on the twins. Then change clothes. Put on something a little less constricting than my jeans."

Frankly, he preferred her in something *more* constricting. Like a suit of armor with a chastity belt. That would be good. But since that wasn't going to happen, he took a breath and got a grip on his rampaging thoughts. What he had to do here was focus on his anger, he told himself firmly. Just remember that she'd lied to him. Hidden his children from him. That should take care of the raging need clawing at him.

"All right, let's go."

She paused and looked up at him. "I can do it myself."

"Sure you can. You're a superhero." He drew her to her feet. "So do me a favor. Stop fighting this so hard. Pretend to need my help. Make me feel manly."

She snorted a laugh. "Like you need help with that."

"I think that was a compliment," he said, following her toward the hall and presumably, her bedroom.

"You don't need a compliment, either."

"Harsh," he said, amused in spite of the conversation. Walking behind her, his gaze dropped to the curve of her behind, defined by the worn, faded denim that clung to her body like a second skin. His body stirred again and he gritted his teeth.

She walked slowly and he could sense the pain that accompanied every movement. Didn't seem to stop the sexual thoughts dancing through his mind. But a part of him admired her steely determination to keep going in spite of whatever pain was gnawing on her. She refused to surrender to it. Refused to give in to what had to be an urge to curl up somewhere and whimper.

Hell, she was stronger than him. When he broke his leg off the coast of Monaco in a car wreck during a race, Colt had bitched about the pain to anyone who would listen.

Even Connor had lost all patience with him by the time his leg had finally healed. But in his defense, Colt thought, he wasn't the kind of guy to be content sitting in a damn chair and watching TV. He needed to be moving. Doing. Chasing risk and searching for that next shot of adrenaline. Life was too short to not try to wring every last drop of pleasure out of it.

Too damn short. Those three words rippled through his mind, dragging up the past from the shadows where he'd hidden it. Smothering a tight groan, Colt shoved that past back down again, refusing to acknowledge it. Refusing to even look at it.

The past was done. What counted was now.

Of course, the past was what had brought him here, to this house, today.

He watched her quietly approach a closed door off the hallway and carefully turn the knob, making no sound as she stepped inside. Colt hesitated, knowing that his children were in there. Emotions choked him as she turned to look at him, a quizzical look on her face.

Colt knew she was expecting him to follow her in and see the twins as they slept. But he wasn't interested in seeing his kids for the first time while in front of an audience. He could wait a bit longer to see the babies who had brought him here. And he'd do it in his own time.

Hell, he realized with a start, he was actually *nervous*. He couldn't even remember the last time he'd felt the skitter of nerves racking his body. Colt had faced down volcanoes, killer surf, parachutes that didn't open and broken skis on the steep face of a so-called un-skiable mountain. Yet the thought of meeting his children for the first time had him backing away from an open doorway as if it were a gateway to some black, dangerous pit.

So he waited while she fiddled with blankets and murmured soft sounds of comfort and love. He was finding it hard to breathe past a knot of sensation that he recognized as it grew inside him. This wasn't nerves. This was a familiar, buzzing feeling settling into the pit of his stomach. He felt it every time he stood at the tip of a mountain, jumped off a cliff, rode forty-foot surf. It was that surge of adrenaline that let him know he was alive.

That he was about to risk it all. About to put his life on the line and either change it—or end it.

He didn't care which.

"Colt?"

She was back in the hall, with the babies' door closed, and she was looking at him. He stared down into those green eyes he'd never really been able to forget. "What?"

"I just thought you'd want to see the twins…"

"I do," he assured her, getting a tight rein on the runaway sensations pouring through him. "Later."

"Okay then." She walked past him slowly, heading to the end of the hall and another closed door. Looking back at him over her shoulder, she reluctantly acknowledged, "You were right before. I think I will need your help getting out of these clothes."

In different circumstances, getting her undressed would have been Colt's highest priority. But things were different now. They weren't lovers. They were…what? Enemies? Maybe. Sure weren't friends. Exes with children. He looked at Penny and saw misery in her eyes and it wasn't hard to identify the reason. Couldn't have been easy for her to admit to him that she needed help. Especially from him. Right now, things between them were strained so tight, the tension in the air between them flavored every breath.

And it wasn't only the situation with the twins that had them each walking a fine line. It was the sexual chemistry still buzzing between them. But chemistry didn't have to be acted on, did it? Nodding, he said, "Fine."

His brain was busy, racing with too many thoughts to sort out, and that was just as well. If he kept his anger burning, he'd be able to ignore the rush of desire already pulsing inside him.

He followed Penny into her bedroom and took a second or two to look around. A full-size bed on one wall, bedside tables and a tall dresser. There were framed photos on the walls—hers, he was willing to bet—of the beach, parks and two smiling babies.

They were beautiful. Both of them. His heart gave an unexpected leap that staggered him. *His* children. Yes, he'd get a paternity test, but just looking at those two faces caught forever and trapped behind glass, he knew they were his. They looked like him. They each had the King black hair and blue eyes and he could see his own features replicated in miniature.

"They look like you," she said softly.

His throat squeezed shut and he could hear his own heartbeat hammering in his ears. He kept his gaze fixed on the photos. It seemed he was going to be seeing his children for the first time in front of an audience after all. "When did you take the pictures?"

"Two weeks ago," she said. "We went to the park, which is why Reid has sand on his face. He tries to eat everything he finds."

A tight smile curved Colt's mouth as he looked at his son's mischievous face. There was a sparkle in the tiny boy's eyes that promised trouble. And his sister had that same flash of something special about her, Colt thought. *His* children. And he didn't know them. Had never heard them. Had never held them. His heart took another leap and he forced himself to turn from the framed photos to the woman sitting on the edge of the bed.

"You cheated me, Penny," he ground out tightly as a fresh surge of anger washed over him. "Nobody cheats a King and gets away with it."

Four

"Cheated you?" she countered, green eyes glittering. "*You* walked away, Colt. You cheated yourself. Out of the kids, out of what we could have had."

Shaking his head, he took a step back from her and tried to keep his voice down in spite of the raging fury inside him. Seeing his kids there on her wall, realizing just how much of their lives he'd already missed, had stoked the fire of his anger until it felt as if he were being consumed.

"Yeah, I walked. From a marriage that was a mistake," he muttered. The past came rushing forward, but he wouldn't look at it. Refused to remember the pain and shock in her eyes as he left her.

"It didn't last long enough to be classified a mistake," she countered.

She was right about that much. Colt reached up and

pushed both hands through his hair. He'd relived his decision to spontaneously get married a million times over the last eighteen months and he still couldn't explain to himself why he'd done it. But in that wild moment in the tacky little chapel, he'd known he wanted her with him for always.

"Always" had lasted about ten hours.

Dawn eventually came and shook him out of the passion-induced haze he'd been operating in. In the glare of morning, he'd remembered at last that "forever" didn't exist. That marriage just wasn't in his game plan—in spite of how amazing he and Penny were in bed together.

He'd believed then, and he still did, that walking away was the right thing to do. But he would have walked right back if she'd even once mentioned the whole pregnancy thing.

"What did you think was going to happen, Penny?" He glared down at her, refusing to be swayed by the gleam in her eyes or the tilt of her chin. "Did you really see us living the suburban dream? Is that it?"

"No," she said on a short laugh. "But—"

"But what? Would it have been better to stay married for a month? Six? And then end it? Would that have seemed kinder," he asked, "or would it just have prolonged the inevitable?"

"I don't know," she muttered, pushing her hair back from her face with an impatient gesture. "All I know is, we dated, got married and got divorced in the span of a week and now you're back claiming that I somehow cheated you."

"It always comes back to the same thing, Penny," he said, voice low and deep. "You should have told me."

She blew out a breath and glared at him. "And here we are again, on the carousel of knives where we just slash at each other and nothing is ever solved."

Colt stalked a few paces away from the bed, but he couldn't get far, since the whole room would have fit inside his walk-in closet. He felt trapped. In the small space. In this situation. But despite the invisible chains wrapping around him tighter by the moment, he knew he couldn't leave. Wouldn't leave. He had children— whether he'd planned on it or not—and he had to do right by them.

He spun around to look at her and promised, "You can't keep me from the twins."

"You'll just confuse them," she told him flatly.

"Confuse them how?" He threw both hands high then let them slap back down against his thighs. "They're babies. They don't know what's going on!"

"Keep your voice down—you'll wake them up." She glared at him and after a second or two of that heated stare, he shifted uncomfortably. "And they understand when people are happy. Or angry. And I don't want you upsetting them by shouting."

Colt took a breath and nodded. "Fine." He lowered his voice because he hadn't meant to shout in the first place. Connor was the twin with the hot temper. Which just went to show how far out of his own comfort zone Colt really was. "Confuse them how?"

"You're a stranger to them—"

He gritted his teeth.

"—and you just pop up into their lives? For how long, Colt? How long before you tell them, 'Sorry kids, but I'm just not father material. I'll have my lawyers contact you about child support.'"

"Funny." His tone was flat, his eyes narrowed and he had a very slight grip on the temper that was beginning to ice over his insides. "You can be as bitter as you want about what happened between us. But I'm not going to do that to them."

"And how do I know that?" She winced as she straightened on the bed. "You walked away from a wife. Why not your kids, too?"

"It's different and you know it."

"No, I don't. That's the problem."

The last of the daylight pearled the room in a warm, pale haze that floated through the open curtains and lay across the oak floor like gold dust. As the old house settled down for the night, it creaked and groaned like a tired old woman settling in for a nap. There was a baby monitor on her bedside table that crackled with static and then broadcast one of the babies coughing.

Colt jolted at the sound. "Are they choking?"

"No," Penny said with a sigh. "That's just Riley. When she sleeps she sucks so hard on her pacifier that she gurgles and coughs."

"Is that normal?" Frowning at the monitor, he felt completely out of his element here. How would he know what was normal for an infant or not? It wasn't as if he spent all that much time with any of the new King babies. Seeing them at family parties hadn't really prepared him for a lot of one-on-one time with two infants.

"Yes. Colt—"

He heard the fatigue in her voice. Saw it in her eyes and the pale color of her skin. They were going around and around and not gaining ground. There would be plenty of time to sort out what they were going to do. And when he argued with someone, he wanted them at full strength. Penny clearly was not. He didn't want to worry about her, but a slender thread of concern drifted through him anyway.

"Let's just get you changed, all right? We'll talk about this more tomorrow."

"Oh, boy," she murmured. "There's something to look forward to." Then she winced and tugged at the snap on her jeans. "But I'm so uncomfortable, I'm willing to risk it."

"What do you need?"

"My nightgown's in the top drawer of the dresser."

Nightgown.

And she'd be naked underneath it, of course. Even as he felt his body stir and tighten, he had to wonder how he could be so furious with a woman and want her so badly all at the same damn time. Still grinding his teeth, he moved to the dresser, opened the top drawer and discovered there actually *was* a cure for lust.

"This? Really?" he asked, holding up the most hideous nightgown he'd ever seen.

She frowned. "And what's wrong with it?"

Shaking his head, he gave her the fire-engine-red sleep shirt that was stamped with oversized, mustard-yellow flowers and hot pink ribbons.

"Other than the fact that it looks radioactive? Not a thing," he mused. "It's probably great birth control. One look at you in this thing and the guy in question runs for the hills."

"Very funny." She snatched it from him. "It was on sale."

"For how many years?" It was the ugliest thing he'd ever seen and he blessed her for having it. Maybe the truly fugly nightgown would help him to *not* think about what was under it.

"I didn't ask you to critique my wardrobe."

"You could ask me to burn your wardrobe," he offered. "Or at least that part of it."

"Could you just—" She pushed one hand through her wild, wavy fall of red hair and pushed it back over her shoulder. "Never mind. I'll do this myself. Just… go away."

"Stop being so stubborn." He wanted to get this over and done with. "I'll help you with the nightgown, but I'll close my eyes to protect my retinas."

She glared at him. "Are you going to help me or just make snide comments?"

"I can do both. Who says men can't multitask?"

"God, you're irritating."

"Nice that you noticed."

He was noticing plenty himself. Too much. Such as the fact that she was trembling—and it wasn't because she was cold, or even furious. She was feeling just what he was. That raw, nerve-scraping need that had pushed them into bed together in the first place. It was something he'd never found with anyone else. Something he'd told himself many times that he just wasn't interested in. Apparently, though, his body had missed that memo.

Frustration practically wafted off her in waves and Colt told himself he really shouldn't be enjoying giving her a hard time so much. But he was owed some payback, right? Besides, it kept his thoughts too busy to entertain *other* things.

"I changed my mind. I can get undressed myself."

"No, you can't. Not yet, anyway." He stepped up in

front of her and when she drew back, he said, "Relax, Penny. I've seen it before, remember?"

God knew *he* remembered. Every square inch of her body was burned into his brain, despite how often he had tried to erase it. "We're both grownups, and believe it or not, I do have some self-control. I'm not going to jump a woman just out of the hospital."

Probably.

She whipped her hair out of her eyes to look at him. "You wouldn't be doing that anyway."

"Is that right?" If she knew just how hard and tight his body was at the moment, she'd be sounding a lot less confident.

Meeting his gaze, she reminded him again, "You're the one who walked away from me, Colt. So why would you want to go back there?"

Why indeed?

Because, damn it, he'd wanted to go back there ever since the moment he'd walked away from her in Vegas. Hell, it's one reason he *had* walked away from her. She made him think too much. Feel too much.

To cover his thoughts he said, "Trust me, once you're wearing that very effective male-repellent nightgown, you'll be safe."

"That's a relief." She didn't sound relieved, though.

"Come on, let's get this done." He moved closer, took the hem of her T-shirt and waited while she pulled her arms from the sleeves. Then he tugged it up and over her head. Her hair fell like red silk, settling over her shoulders. And if he kept his gaze on her hair, he'd be fine. Yeah, it was touchable but not nearly as hard to resist as the lace bra cupping her generous breasts. He drew in a shallow breath and waited while she unhooked the front clasp, then shrugged the bra off.

Modestly, she crossed her arms over her breasts, but the action was pointless. The quick look he'd gotten was enough to make him hard again, and he had the feeling that he'd better get used to that particular kind of misery.

To help himself as much as her, Colt tugged the nightgown over her head and took a step back as she pushed her arms through the sleeves and drew the hideous fabric down over her body. He'd called that nightshirt a man repellent—apparently he was immune.

She toed off her sneakers, then reached under the nightgown to unsnap her jeans. Once she'd pulled the zipper down, Colt stepped in again. "Lie back. I'll get them off you."

She did, but she braced herself on her elbows and kept a wary eye on him as he drew the denim down and off her long, well-toned legs. Smothering a groan, he tried not to think about those legs wrapped around his waist, pulling him closer, deeper. Tried not to remember the sound of her sighs or the flex of her muscles as she writhed beneath him. And he was failing.

Miserably.

"Okay," he said, taking a deliberate step back. "Finished."

"Thanks." Nodding, she eased into a sitting position and tugged her nightgown down over her thighs.

Good thing, too, he told himself. Because he was on the ragged edge of control, and that edge was crumbling underneath his feet. The anger still simmering inside him didn't seem to have an effect on the pulse of desire that kicked into high gear whenever he was close to her.

Hell, the woman could still turn his body to stone without an effort.

Thankfully, his heart had turned to stone ten years ago, so that particular organ was in no danger.

"I think," Penny said, drawing him back to the moment at hand, "I'll just lie down for a minute or two."

"Yeah. Good idea. Do you still drink that disgusting green tea?"

Surprise flickered in her eyes. "Yes."

He gave a shudder but said, "I'll make you some."

Colt left her staring after him and got out of her bedroom as quickly as he could. No point in torturing himself, watching Penny stretch out across a bed he really wanted to join her in. Frowning at his own train of thought, he reminded himself that he and Penny were done. The only reason he was here now was to see the twins. To make sure they were safe. Being cared for.

When he left her room, he fully intended to go straight to the kitchen. Instead, he stopped outside the twins' bedroom. He laid one hand on the old-fashioned brass knob and felt the cool metal bite into his skin. His heartbeat jumped into a gallop and every breath came fast and shallow.

He felt the way he had the first time he'd gone paragliding in the Alps. That wild mixture of excitement, dread and sheer blind panic that made a man so grateful to be back on the ground when it was all over, he wanted to kiss the dirt. But just as on that long-ago day, there was no turning back. He had to jump off the side of that mountain. Had to take this next step into a future he never would have predicted.

Opening the door quietly, he stepped inside. Colt heard them before he saw them. Quick, soft breaths, a muffled whimper and a scooting sound as one of them shifted in their sleep. Colt scrubbed one hand across the back of his neck and walked silently across the dimly lit room. Outside, the sun was setting, casting a few last, lingering rays through a window that overlooked a tiny backyard.

Inside, there were two white cribs, angled so that the twins could see each other when they woke. There was a rocking chair in one corner of the room, shelves for toys and books, and matching dressers standing at attention against one wall. Pictures in brightly colored frames dotted the walls and at a glance, Colt could see the photos were of rainbows and parks and animals…everything that would make a baby smile.

But it was the babies he was interested in. His footsteps were quiet, and still the old wood floor creaked with his movements. But the twins didn't react; they slept on, dreaming. Taking a deep breath, Colt steadied himself, then walked up to stand between the cribs, where he could see each of his children.

Riley wore pink pajamas and slept on her stomach, arms curled, hands beneath her, tiny behind pointed skyward. He smiled and looked at twin number two. Reid's black hair was trimmed shorter than his sister's. He wore pale green pajamas and slept sprawled on his back, arms and impossibly short legs spread out as though he were making a snow angel. Both of them were so beautiful, so small, so…fragile, they stole his heart in a blink.

He didn't need a paternity test to be sure they were his. Instinctively, he knew they were his children. He *felt* it. There was a thread of connection sliding through him, binding him to each of them. Colt reached out his hands and curled a fist around the top rail of the matching cribs. His heart might be stone where women were concerned, but these babies had already stamped themselves on his soul. Each whispered breath tightened the invisible thread joining them and in a few short moments, Colt knew he would do anything for them.

But first, he had to deal with their mother.

Penny woke up, disoriented at first. A quick glance at her surroundings told her she was at home and she took a relieved breath, grateful to be out of the hospital.

"The twins!" Her eyes went wide as she realized that watery morning sunlight was creeping through her bedroom window. She'd slept all night. Hadn't seen the babies since that one quick check the night before. Hadn't heard a thing. What if they had cried out for her? How could she sleep so soundly that for the first time in eight months, she hadn't heard them?

Pushing herself out of bed, she took two hurried steps toward the door before the pain in her abdomen slowed her movements to a more cautious speed. She went to the twins' room and stopped in the doorway. The cribs were empty. Her heart pounded so hard against her ribs she could hardly breathe. Panic shot through her still-sleep-fogged mind.

Then she heard it.

A deep voice, *Colt's* voice, sounded low, gentle, and her initial bout of panic edged away to be replaced by a wary tenderness.

Penny followed his voice, moving slowly, cautiously, through the house that had been hers for the last two years. The house that was still filled with memories from her own childhood. The house where she'd made a home for her kids.

At the kitchen doorway, she paused, unnoticed by the three people in the room. The twins were in their high chairs, slapping tiny palms against trays that held gleefully mushed scrambled eggs. Their father—Colt—sat opposite them, talking, teasing, laughing when Reid threw a small fistful of egg at him. Penny's heart ached and throbbed. She used to dream about seeing Colt like this with the twins. Used to fantasize about what it would be like for the four of them to be a family.

And for one quick moment, she allowed herself the luxury of living in that fantasy. Of believing that somehow, the last eighteen months had been written differently. That Colt belonged here. With them. With *her*.

"Are you going to come in or just stand there watching?"

She jolted as he turned his head to spear her with a look. Guilt rushed through her and the fantasy died a quick, necessary death. What was the point in torturing herself, after all, when she knew that Colt didn't want her? All he wanted was her children. And the twins, he couldn't have.

"I didn't think you knew I was here."

"I can feel your disapproval from here."

She flushed again and moved into the room. When the twins spotted her, there were squeals of welcome and her heart thrilled to it. She went first to one, then the other, planting kisses and inhaling that wonderful baby scent that clung to each of them. She took a seat close by and watched as Colt continued feeding the babies, dipping a spoon into peach yogurt again and again, distributing it between the twins, who held their mouths open like baby birds.

"You got them up and dressed," she said, noting the fresh shirts and pants, the little socks on their tiny feet.

"You sound surprised," he said.

"I guess I am." In fact, she was stunned. She'd thought that Colt would be lost dealing with the twins. Instead, he had them changed and fed and was behaving as if he always started out his mornings in a three-ring circus.

He never stopped feeding the babies as he spoke. "The King family has been procreating at a phenomenal rate the last few years." He shrugged. "You can't go to any family gathering without someone handing you a baby who needs changing or feeding or both. So I've had plenty of practice. We all have. Granted, I don't spend a lot of time with the babies…but enough to know my way around a diaper."

True. He'd told her about all the children his cousins were having. She just had never once considered that he would have taken any interest in them. As he'd told her himself, Colt wasn't the family type. He was more interested in risking his life than in living it.

"Still," he mused, his voice tightening slightly, "I've never done it for my own kids before." He shot her a sideways look that was hard and cold and promised a long talk in the very near future.

"Colt…" She was too tired, too achy to deal with him.

Where Colt was concerned, nothing was easy—except the passion. That had been cataclysmic from the start. From the very first moment they'd met, their eyes had locked and a chemistry like she'd never felt before had burst into life, burning away every inhibition, every ounce of logic, even her most ingrained natural defenses.

Everything she thought she knew about herself had drained away in the face of the overwhelming pull of the magnetism drawing her and Colt together. So she'd let it go. Everything she'd ever believed. Everything she'd ever promised herself. She had surrendered completely to what her body was demanding—and when it was over, when Colt walked away, she'd paid the price.

She wouldn't make the same mistake twice. So whatever he had to say to her, she would fight him. She would stand strong against that wild feeling of raw passion because she knew that it didn't last. She'd lived it.

"I think they're finished," he said abruptly, cutting off her thoughts. He stood, got a paper towel damp and wiped two happy little faces and sets of grubby fingers. While he did, he asked, "You want to tell me about them?" He paused. "Or is that a secret, too?"

She swallowed hard and stood, unbuckling Riley and lifting the baby into her arms. The twinge of pain was worth it to feel her daughter's solid warmth pressed against her. Kissing the baby's cheek, she said, "What do you want to know?"

"Everything, Penny," he murmured, lifting Reid free of his seat. "I've discovered some things on my own in the last couple of hours with them—"

"Tell me," she said, wondering what he thought of the children he'd only just met.

"Well, for one thing, Reid's going to be left-handed. And he's already got a pretty good arm on him." Colt held the little boy easily in the crook of his arm and grinned when Reid patted both of his cheeks. "And I've figured out that Riley is the more adventurous one. She doesn't like being held for too long. She wants to be on the floor, getting into things. Reid likes cuddling, but he's more than willing to join his sister to plow through a room."

Penny laughed shortly. It was such an apt description

of the twins. Reid was thoughtful contemplation and Riley was a trailblazer. "You're right. I always thought Riley was the most like you."

One black eyebrow lifted and he shook his head. "When we were little, Con was the one off pushing envelopes. I wanted to be near my mom—and the cookie supply."

She smiled at the image of Colt as a cookie-stealing little boy, but had to ask, "Then why are you the one who flies off to adventure spots while Connor runs your business from an office?"

The light in his eyes dimmed, then went out completely as his features shuttered, effectively sealing her out of whatever he was feeling. "Things change."

Penny felt as though she'd struck a nerve, but she had no idea how. King's Extreme Adventures was so well-known that everyone was aware of which twin was the crazy one. The week they were together, Colt had told her stories about his travels for the company.

And most of those stories had terrified her. Being helicoptered in to ski down the sheer face of a mountain? Climbing to the rim of a volcano where the heat of the magma was so intense, you were forced to wear protective heat suits? Parasailing in the Alps. Chasing tornadoes. He'd done them all and more and he seemed to thrive on not only the adventure—but the risk.

And as much as she'd loved him, as much as it had pained her to watch him walk away, she'd had to admit to herself that they never would have worked out anyway. How could she love a man who thought nothing of putting his life on the line in exchange for a brief shot of adrenaline? And now, how could she allow her kids to love a father who was so careless with his own life that one day he wasn't going to come home?

"You're right." Penny carried Riley into the living room and heard Colt following after her. His footsteps were loud against the wood floor and seemed to mimic the thump of her own heart. Having him here in the home she'd made was…distracting.

She had to find a way to get him out again. "Some things do change," she said, carefully easing the baby onto the floor beside a huge plastic toy bin. She took off the lid and smiled as Riley pulled herself up to wobble unsteadily, a wide, proud smile on her face.

Penny took a seat on the nearby sofa and watched as Colt set Reid down beside his sister. But rather than sitting down with her, Colt moved to the front window and glanced outside at the morning sunlight before turning to face her again.

Judging by the expression on his face, Penny knew they were about to have that "talk" he'd been promising her. And frankly, she was ready for it. Get everything out in the open so he could go away and she and her twins could have their lives back.

"You should have told me." The words dropped into the silence like stones plunked into a well.

She took a breath and prepared for battle. "I get that you're angry."

He snorted. "You think?"

She met his gaze from across the room, refusing to be cowed or ashamed of the decision she'd made. "You made it plain, that last morning in Vegas, that you didn't want to be married and you definitely didn't want kids."

His mouth tightened into a grim line and a muscle in his jaw twitched. "Yeah, I did say that," he admitted.

"But that was hypothetical kids. Did I ever say that if you were pregnant I wouldn't want to know about it?"

"You might as well have." Penny shifted on the sofa carefully, her stitches pulling and aching, reminding her that she wasn't at her best. "I knew that you wouldn't care."

"So you're a mind reader." He nodded sagely.

"I didn't have to read your mind, Colt. You said it all. Flat out in plain English," she argued, not willing to stand there and take sole responsibility for what had happened between them. "You walked out on me, Colt. Why did I owe you anything?"

"You had my *children*." His voice lowered, emphasizing that last word without having to shout.

She stiffened and he must have noticed because he took a breath, seemed to settle himself and then said, "All right. Let's start over. Just tell me *why* you didn't tell me when you first found out you were pregnant."

"I already told you." What she didn't add was that she had also been afraid. Afraid of the King name, the King fortune. She'd worried that he might simply turn his lawyers loose and take her children from her. And he'd pretty much threatened to do just that when he first stormed back into her life. What chance would she have had against the kind of power the Kings could muster?

"I missed a hell of a lot, Penny, and I'm not forgetting that anytime soon."

"I understand." Which meant, of course, that she and Colt were on opposite sides of this battle and unless they found a way to build a bridge across the gap separating them, there would be no solution. No peace. "You know about them now, Colt. What are you going to do about it?"

He pushed one hand through his hair and she remembered that impatient gesture. "I don't know," he grumbled and shot a quick look at the twins, babbling happily at each other. "All I'm sure of is I want to know them."

She could understand that and, maybe, a small part of her warmed to him because of it. But the fact was that Penny was still exhausted, sore and not a little off her game since Colt had walked back into her life. So being cool and logical was a stretch at the moment.

Walking around the couch, he took a seat in a chair opposite her and close to the twins. His gaze shifted to them briefly and Penny watched his features soften. When he looked back to her, though, his eyes were chips of ice again. "I won't be a stranger to my own kids, Penny. I won't be shut out of their lives."

A sinking sensation swamped her as she came to grips with her new reality. Whether she liked it or not, Colt would be a part of her children's lives. Now she had to find a way to protect them from caring for him too much. Because though he insisted he wanted to be a part of their world right now, she knew that wouldn't last long. How could it? He was always traveling, wandering the world, looking for the next rush.

Taking a deep breath, she said, "And what about the next time you go wingsuit flying? Or parasailing?"

He frowned. "What're you talking about?"

"You, Colt," she said. "It's just not in your nature to be a suburban dad. You won't last a month before you'll be off running with bulls or some other crazy thing."

"Crazy?"

"Yes. You risk your life all the time and you do it because you like it." She shook her head. "I saw pictures of you in a magazine last month—standing on the rim of a volcano while magma jumped in the air around you."

"Yeah. I was in Japan scouting new sites. So?"

"So how's a quiet street in Laguna going to hold your interest, Colt?" She gave him a small smile. "This isn't your world. Never will be. Why fight so hard to be a part of something you never wanted in the first place?"

His gaze never left the twins. Reid plopped down onto his behind and Riley leaned over to pull a car from her brother's grasp. Reid's face screwed up as he prepared to howl, but Colt cut off the reaction by reaching into the plastic tub and getting another car that he handed to Reid. Immediately, the baby looked up at him and gave his father a wide enough smile that all three of his teeth were displayed.

Colt laughed a little, waited another moment or two and then shifted his gaze to hers. "Because, Penny. I'm a King. And to a King, family is everything."

Five

Penny's fists curled into the fabric of her nightgown and held on as if it meant her life. And in a way, it did. The tangible, very real feel of what Colt had called her "radioactive" nightshirt reminded her of who she was and where she was. This was her home and he was the intruder. For the moment at least, they were on her turf and she held all the cards.

How long *that* would last, she couldn't even guess.

Even from across the room, she felt the magnetic pull of him and had to fight against it. He wasn't here for her—he was here to rip apart her world.

Pain ripped through her and she hated knowing that he still had the ability to hurt her. She'd worked so hard to get past this. To get over Colton King. And she'd done a pretty good job of it, too. She hardly ever thought of him anymore—well, no more than a few times a day and all night in her dreams—but now he was here again, back in her life. This was going to reset her starting-over clock and soon she'd be going through all the misery she'd already survived once. But better to do it now, she told herself. While the kids were too little to understand. Too small to remember him. To miss him when he was gone.

But their argument was circular. He blamed her for keeping secrets. She blamed him for walking away. There was no middle ground here, so she'd have to try to create some.

"Colt, I get what you're trying to do."

"Is that right?"

"But," she said, ignoring the taunt, "you don't have to. Just because they're your family doesn't mean you have to *be* here."

Nodding slowly, he fixed his gaze on hers and she could have sworn she felt the temperature in the room drop a few degrees. "Where should I be?"

She threw her hands up, already forgetting about that calm, cool middle ground she was going to build. Panic wasn't a good breeding ground for calm and cool. "I don't know. Bali? Australia? The top of a mountain, or the bottom of the sea?"

"You're wrong. I should be right here."

"No, I'm not wrong." A short, sharp laugh escaped her. "Right now, you're doing what you think you should, Colt. Not what you want to do. And when this rush of responsibility has faded, you'll take off again. It's what you do. It's who you are."

Riley chose that moment to crawl to her father and pull herself up by grabbing tiny fistfuls of his jeans. She staggered a little and swayed more than a few times, but Colt sat perfectly still, watching his daughter grow and develop right before his eyes. Her black hair curled around her ears, her blue eyes shone with happiness and her chubby hands slapped at his legs in triumph as she finally found her feet.

He covered one tiny hand with his and stroked his thumb over Riley's smooth skin. Penny's foolish, gullible heart gave a ping of tenderness at what she was seeing and just for a second or two, she caught a glimpse of *what might have been.*

Finally, Colt looked at her again. "I'm here. Whether you like it or not, and you're just going to have to deal with my presence."

Not for long, she promised herself, determined not to be touched by the gentle way he treated the twins. Not to be swayed by the warmth in his eyes. She'd been fooled once by Colton King. She'd believed that he had felt the same way she had—swept away by a powerful and unexpected swell of love. And she'd been crushed. Devastated.

In fact, the only thing that had held her together after signing his divorce papers was finding out she was pregnant.

Knowing that she would have a child—then two— helped her to refocus her life. To concentrate the love she'd thought she'd lost onto two children who had become the very center of her life.

She wouldn't allow Colt to hurt her again. Or worse, to hurt the twins with his callous disinterest in real, honest feelings.

"I'm here. Deal with it," Colt told her, his voice steely with determination. "Besides, you're just out of the hospital and you need help, whether you want to admit it or not."

She wanted to argue, but the pain in her abdomen made that impossible. Looking up at Colt, Penny had to admit, at least to herself, that she wasn't going to win this one. And if she kept arguing, she'd only end up looking like an idiot. She was in no shape to take care of herself, let alone the twins. Colt was right. She did need help.

She just didn't want to need *him*.

Still, he was here and maybe… She nearly smiled as something occurred to her. Maybe if Colt was here, in the middle of what was Penny's normal chaotic life, if he could experience firsthand just how much work two babies could be, he would leave that much sooner.

Right now, she knew he was running on anger and regret that he was only now finding out about the twins. But sooner or later, his natural inclination to take off would kick in. He might not be able to admit it to himself, but Penny knew that even now, that itch was gnawing at him. If she let him stay, let him take care of the twins, it might be enough to push him away that much faster. And though it pained her to think of him leaving again, she knew it was for the best that it happened fast.

"Okay," she said.

"Okay what?" He looked at her, suspicion gleaming in his eyes.

"Okay, you're right. I do need help and you *are* the twins' father."

"Uh-huh." If anything, his eyes narrowed even further.

She gave him a smile that cost her some of her pride. "Don't look so surprised. You convinced me, that's all."

"Is that right?"

Penny sighed. "Colt, you wanted me to agree with you and I have."

"That's what worries me," he admitted quietly, his suspicious gaze still locked on her.

Reid crawled at top speed across the floor to join his sister. Grabbing hold of Colt's jeans, he pulled himself up, and laughed in delight as he and Riley took turns slapping their palms against Colt's thigh. For a minute or two, he simply watched them, a smile curving his mouth, and when he looked over at Penny again, that smile was still reflected in his eyes.

She felt a way-too-familiar jolt of something that she knew was dangerous. Attraction mingled with old feelings of love that were already being rekindled. But she didn't want that fire again. Didn't want to get burned by her own emotions being tossed at the feet of a man who had already made it clear that he didn't want them.

But she knew there was no way to stop what she felt for Colt. The only remedy would be to get him to leave as soon as possible. Then she could lose herself in her kids and her work and pretend that there wasn't a large, gaping wound in her heart.

The next morning, after a hideously sleepless night, thanks to red-hot dreams of Colt, Penny stood in the bathroom studying her reflection in the mirror. Right away, she really wished she had simply draped a towel over the mirror instead.

Her hair was wild, her face looked pale and she really wanted a shower but didn't think she'd be able to manage it on her own. And frankly, the thought of asking Colt for help with *that* problem was too much to consider. Just thinking about being wet and slippery with Colt's hands moving over her soap-slicked body made her want to whimper with need. Which was just enough to make her push aside the fantasy and deal with reality.

He'd stormed into her life and was so busy laying claim to everything around her that Penny felt as though she had to make a stand.

Frowning, she let her gaze drop. All right, yes, her nightgown wasn't the most attractive piece of clothing she'd ever owned, but it was *hers*. Just as this house, these kids, were *hers*. And as for the nightgown being a man repellent, maybe she should have it tattooed onto her skin. But that would only take care of keeping Colt away from her. She couldn't think of a thing to keep *her* from wanting him. Except, of course, that large dose of reality. Too bad that whenever she was around Colt she tended to do more feeling than thinking.

Shaking her head at the sad, sad woman in the mirror, Penny brushed her hair, washed her face and then got dressed. A long-sleeved green T-shirt over some comfy old jeans and she thought she was ready to face Colt.

Naturally, she couldn't have been more wrong.

"What are you *doing?*" She walked into the kitchen, a little steadier on her feet, thank heaven, than she had been the day before. But what she found in the kitchen had her swaying. In indignation. Colt sat at her small round table, her laptop open in front of him and stacks of unpaid bills laid out around him.

Humiliation was a living, breathing thing inside her. With this latest invasion of her privacy, she felt as if he'd stripped her bare and she was so furious about it, she was practically vibrating.

Colt barely glanced up from her computer. "I'm paying your bills."

"You can't do that," she managed to say through gritted teeth.

"Sure I can. All you need is money and I've got plenty."

Another verbal slap—another reminder of just how different their lives were—and she felt it right down to her bones. He was a King. He had more money than she could ever dream of and here he was, tossing it in her face. Just to make sure she knew where she stood in this particular battle.

He looked so confident, so sure of himself, sitting there in a slice of sunlight while the twins happily feasted on the Cheerios scattered across their tray tables.

"I don't care how much money you have, Colt." Lies, lies. If he were poor, she wouldn't be so worried about what he could do to her life. But no, he just *had* to be one of the richest men in California. "I pay *my* bills with *my* money."

One black eyebrow quirked. "Not lately, you haven't."

Her gaze swept the embarrassingly tall stack of bills that he slapped one big hand on top of.

"Things have been a little slow lately businesswise, but it's about to pick up." Defensively, she folded her arms across her chest. "Just butt out, Colt."

"Nope, can't do it," he said, lifting his gaze to hers at last.

His features were cold, hard, and his eyes glinted like chips of ice in the sun. He looked out of place in her bright, sage-green kitchen with its yellow cabinets and old scarred floors.

"By the looks of this mess, you're in deep and sinking fast."

Who knew there was *more* humiliation to be felt,

Penny thought. Lying awake nights worrying about how to pay her bills was her business. She hated that now he knew all about it, too. With no other choice in how to handle the situation, she stiffened her spine, lifted her chin and did what she always did when she was faced with immutable facts. She brazened her way through.

"I'm building a business," she argued. "That takes time. Something you wouldn't know about, I'm guessing, because the Kings don't have to actually *work* for a living."

Inwardly, she winced at the snide tone in her voice. She even knew that what she said wasn't true. But more than that, waving a red flag in front of an already-raging bull was never a good idea. Still, was she supposed to simply stand there and be made to feel like a failure?

As she watched, the chips of ice in his eyes grew flintier. More forbidding. "The Kings have money, yeah," he said, every word covered in frost. "But we're expected to work. To build our businesses, and we *do*. Every last damn one of us works our asses off and we're good at it."

She flushed. "I know. But you don't know what it's like to do it all *alone,* do you?"

He took a breath, scrubbed one hand across his face, then nodded. "Fine. You might have a point." His gaze fixed on hers, he added, "But that's only more reason you should have contacted me. I would've helped."

"That's what you don't get. I didn't *want* your help," she reminded him and realized that she sounded like a whiny child.

Irritated at herself as well as him, she crossed the room in a flash and grabbed for the closest pile of papers.

Colt was faster. He snatched them up and flipped

through them with a casual ease that made her even more furious.

"Electric, gas, phone, cable…" He paused and looked up at her. "Credit cards. You were behind on all of them."

"I make payments," she said, embarrassment tangling with outrage and getting lost in the shuffle.

"Does the phrase 'paid in full' mean anything to you?" he asked, voice quiet, controlled.

"Not really. I pay them what I can when I can."

"Well, now you don't owe anyone," he said flatly.

It would have been really wrong of her to actually experience a sweep of relief, so of course, she didn't allow herself to feel anything like that at all.

"Except *you*," she pointed out and felt the heavy weight of that little fact settle onto her shoulders.

She really was going to have to kill Robert, she told herself firmly. And her brother probably suspected that was her plan since he hadn't come around in a while. If he hadn't gone to Colt none of this would be happening.

"You already owe me," he said, bringing her up out of her thoughts.

"For *what?*" He'd already swept her ordinary world into oblivion. What more could he possibly expect from her?

He just stared at her as silence grew and thickened in the air between them. "Time. I lost eight months with the twins. And the nine months you were pregnant. I didn't see their birth. Didn't see their first smiles or see them crawl for the first time." He shook his head slowly, his gaze still pinning her like a bug to a board. "So don't pretend you don't know what I'm talking about. You kept my children from me, Penny. I'm not forgetting that."

"Neither am I," she said softly, as a flicker of shame

joined the tumult of emotions rattling around inside her. She still believed she'd done the right thing, but seriously, the way Colt had reacted to the news of the twins' existence had really surprised her. She hadn't thought he'd be interested enough to come and see them, let alone stay there, in the house, taking care of two babies who could bring a grown man to his knees.

But even as she thought it, she knew that his actions now didn't mean he would stay.

"That doesn't mean you get to stick your nose into every aspect of my life. How I live is none of your business, Colt."

"It is when it concerns *my* children," he countered neatly. "I looked through your bills because your brother told me you didn't have health insurance. I was worried about the twins. But it seems *they're* covered and those payments are up to date."

"Of course they are," she told him hotly, making another grab for the papers he held in his hand. "I would never take chances with the twins' health."

"But you do with your own."

"I never get sick."

One black eyebrow lifted again and his gaze dropped meaningfully to the fresh scar on her abdomen, now hidden beneath her T-shirt.

Her eyes rolled practically to the back of her head. "Appendicitis is something different. That could happen to anyone."

"Which is why we have health insurance," he said, tone so calm and patient she wanted to shriek.

"I can take care of myself, Colt. I've been doing it most of my life—" She closed her mouth fast before she said more than she wanted to about that. Her past wasn't the point here anyway. Staring at the pile of bills he still held in one tight fist, she thought of something else to throw at him, as well. "You had no right to pay off my hospital bill, either."

"Again," he pointed out, "someone had to."

"But that someone doesn't have to be *you*."

Two days, she told herself. He'd been back in her world about two days and already, things were turned upside down. She didn't want to be indebted to him and if he kept this up, she'd never be able to repay him.

"This cottage is paid for—that's good," he was saying. "But when I took the twins into the yard this morning, I noticed you need a new roof."

"Yes, it's on my list and I'll get to it as soon as I can." That list was miles long though, and the roof was much closer to the bottom of that list than the top. With any luck, rain would be scarce again this winter and she wouldn't have to worry about the roof for another year.

"The roofer will be here on Friday," he said.

Control, like a single, slippery thread, was sliding out of her hands and Penny kept grasping at it fruitlessly. Colton King was a tank. A gorgeous, sexy tank. He simply mowed over whoever or whatever stood in his way, flattening everything in his path.

And she knew that he would do the very same to her if she tried to stand between him and the twins. But what kind of mother would she be if she didn't try to protect her kids from having their little hearts broken? No. She had to hold her ground, not give him another inch, or he would completely take over her life.

"You can't buy me a new roof," she said, keeping her voice quiet and her tone even.

"Already done." He stacked the now-paid bills on

the other side of the computer, where she couldn't reach them easily. Then he leaned back in his chair, folded his arms over his chest and said, "I called my cousin Rafe. His construction crew will be out here on Friday. They're checking for termites while they're at it, since these old cottages are like an all-you-can-eat buffet for those bugs—"

"Dam— Darn it, Colt," she corrected herself quickly with a guilty glance at the babies sitting close by. They would be talking soon and she didn't want them picking up the wrong words. "I don't want you doing this."

"When the first rain hits, you'll thank me," he assured her.

When she first woke up this morning, Penny had actually felt better. Less sore, less tired. Now, she felt as though she needed to go back to bed. If she slept long enough, maybe he would be gone when she woke up again. But even as that idle wish floated through her mind, she set it free because she knew it wouldn't be that easy. Colt wouldn't leave until he was good and ready. And when he did go, there would be no stopping him.

Drawing out the chair beside him, she eased down into it and looked him dead in the eye. "You can't just come into my life and reorder it to suit yourself."

"I paid some bills," he said. "You obviously need the money and I can afford it, so what's the big deal?"

"The big deal is that I pay my own way." Silently, she gave herself a cheer for remaining very cool and logical. "I take care of myself and my family."

He looked at her through serious, cool blue eyes. "But that's the thing, isn't it? The twins are *my* family, too."

Her heart iced over and her stomach sank. This is what she'd been afraid of. That Colt would find out about the twins and immediately claim them. Brush her aside—or steamroller her—and take what he wanted.

A bank of clouds rushed across the sun, sending an intermittent mix of light and shadow into the kitchen. The twins were babbling happily to each other and for the first time, Penny didn't wonder what they were saying, or if they could understand each other. She was too busy trying to understand the subtext of what Colt was saying.

Was he laying claim to his children? Was he already laying the groundwork for pushing Penny out of her babies' lives? Fear became a knot in the center of her chest. For most of her life, she'd taken care of herself. She'd solved her own problems, made her own happiness. Now her life was suddenly out of her control and she didn't have a clue how to deal with it. The one thing she did know was that she wouldn't surrender. Not without a fight.

She kept her voice low and calm when she asked, "Colt, what is it you're after? Just tell me flat out what you expect to happen."

He leaned in toward her, flashed a quick look at the babies, then shifted his gaze back to her. Cloud shadow moved over his features, making his eyes look more distant, more...mysterious.

"I expect my kids to be well taken care of. To have what they need."

"They do," she argued in a choked whisper. Hadn't she been working herself nonstop to ensure just that? She might be a little late on her bills, but they all would have been paid. Eventually. And her kids didn't want for anything. "The twins are healthy and they're *happy*."

She reached out and laid one hand on his forearm. She let him go again instantly and regretted touching him at all, because a zing of reaction shot from her hand, up her arm, to ricochet around the inside of her chest like a ball of heat. That overpowering attraction they'd shared right from the start was obviously alive and well and now throbbing deep inside her. Ignoring her body's clamoring need, she swore, "They'll never go without."

"You're right about that," he said and leaned back in his chair again. He looked every inch a King—in name and profession—lounging comfortably as if he hadn't a care in the world. While Penny sat opposite him, her stomach churning, her mind racing.

This was what it was to be as wealthy as God, she told herself. Colt was so used to being able to command whatever he wanted done, he didn't even think about it. He'd ordered a new roof for her house as easily as she bought a gallon of milk.

Somehow, over the last eighteen months, she'd managed to forget that easy arrogance he carried with him. She'd forgotten that his way of life was so different from hers that they might as well have lived on different planets.

"Don't try to fight me on this, Penny," he warned. "You'll lose."

"Don't be so sure," she countered with more confidence than she felt. What could she possibly do in a battle with one of the Kings of California? He had a fleet of lawyers at his beck and call and a bank account that was endless. If this ended up going to court, then she didn't stand a chance against him and she knew it. So what she had to do was make sure it never went before a judge. She couldn't trust that the courts would choose a mother's love over a father who could support the twins so easily.

"Really?" he asked, clearly amused. "You think you can take me on?"

Oh, there was more than one meaning to that question. She knew, because her body started buzzing and heat sizzled in his eyes, melting the ice. Penny dropped her gaze from his because she didn't want him to see what he could do to her so easily. She only wished it was as simple to hide her reactions from herself.

"I've done something else this morning that you should probably know about," he said.

She swallowed hard, hoping her voice wouldn't sound choked when she said, "What's left?"

"You know your bills are all current now, but I've also transferred money into your bank account—"

"You what?"

He smiled. "I transferred money into your account."

Her blood pressure had to be through the roof because she could actually *hear* her heartbeat in her ears. "How much money?"

One eyebrow lifted. "Greedy?"

"Appalled," she corrected.

He shrugged. "Most women would be delighted to have a half million dollars dropped into their bank accounts."

Six

"A half—" Penny gulped noisily and then blinked as the room spun around her. Her vision narrowed, black rushing in from the edges even as little dark dots danced merrily in front of her. "Half. Half…"

"Breathe, Penny," he suggested.

She wished she could, but her lungs weren't working. Shock had her blinking furiously trying to clear her vision even as she slapped one hand to her chest as if she could somehow jump-start a heart that had clearly stopped. The man was insane. And pushy. And generous. And infuriating.

She opened and closed her mouth on words that wouldn't come. Gasping now, Penny knew she was going to end this "conversation" in a dead faint.

"Damn it," he muttered, then leaned out, put his hand on the back of her head and pushed her forward, until her head was between her knees. "Breathe before you pass out."

She drew in breath after breath and still her chest felt tight and her head was spinning. Penny felt him thread his fingers through her hair, and his touch sent new nerves skittering along her spine. Wasn't it enough that he'd sent her brain into a tailspin? Did he have to do the same to her body? His closeness wasn't making it any easier to breathe.

As if from a distance, she heard the twins laughing and she fought hard against the dizzying sensation clouding her head. Thankfully, they were too young to know just what exactly their daddy could do to their mommy.

When she was able to draw a few deep breaths, she forced herself to say, "Fine. I'm fine, let me up." Once she was sitting up again, she took another breath for good measure and met his gaze. She scowled at the humor glinting in his eyes. Of course he would be enjoying this.

"Good to know I can still make a woman faint."

"You're being *funny?*"

He shrugged casually, but his eyes remained sharp and fixed on her. "I'm not joking when I say they're my kids and I'm going to make sure they're taken care of."

"By buying off their mother?" Insult slapped at her. Did he really believe he could just walk in here, wave his money in front of her face and she'd do backflips to please him? "A half a million dollars? What were you thinking?"

"That you need the money."

"I don't want it, Colt," she said tightly.

"Want it or not, it's done," he said and closed the laptop with a soft click. "You don't have to live from month to month, Penny."

"I don't need your handouts." Okay, big lie. She did need it. She just didn't *want* to need it. A half a million dollars? That was nuts. Just insane. And served to point out once again just how different their lives were.

A flash of heat singed the ice in his eyes. "It's not a handout. It's the right thing to do."

"According to you," she snapped.

"My vote's the only one that counts."

"So typical," she muttered, shaking her head as if trying to convince herself that this was all some kind of nightmare and all she had to do was wake up.

"What's that supposed to mean?"

"It means, you're the one who decided our marriage was a mistake." Words so hard to say. She could still feel the pain of that last morning with him in Vegas. The memory of his eyes, cool, distant, staring at her as if he was watching a stranger. The clipped note in his voice. The fact that he never once looked back as he walked away from her. "Your vote was the only one that counted then, too, I remember."

His features went cold and hard. His eyes took on that same distance she recalled so well. "That was then. This is now. And the sooner you get used to this," he was saying, "the easier it'll be. On all of us."

She pushed to her feet, gave a quick look to the twins, forced a smile for their sakes, then turned back to Colt. "Why should I want to make this easy on *you?* You barged in here and took over. No matter what you think, I'm not your *duty,* Colt. I'm not your *anything*."

His smile was tight, his eyes narrowed as he looked past her briefly to the two babies still happily babbling. "This isn't about you, Penny. It's about them. And the twins are my duty. My responsibility. And I'm going to do whatever I think is right to make sure they have everything they need."

"What they need is love and they have that."

He snorted and tapped his fingers on the thick pile of newly paid bills. "Love doesn't buy groceries or pay the electric company."

She flushed but it was as much anger as it was embarrassment. Penny hated that he knew how tight money was for her. Hated knowing that he was able, with a few clicks of a mouse, to clear away the bills that had been plaguing her. Hated that it was a relief to have that particular worry off her shoulders.

Mostly though, she hated being this close to Colton again because it reminded her that wanting what you couldn't have was just an exercise in self-torture.

"I don't need a white knight in a black SUV riding to the rescue."

"You sure as hell need something, Penny."

"Don't curse in front of the twins."

He stared at her. "They're eight months old. I don't think they're listening to us."

"You have no idea what they hear or remember."

Grumbling under his breath, he pushed back from the table, the chair legs scraping against the wood floor. When he stood up, he walked past her, across the room, heading for the coffeepot. Along the way, he trailed his fingers across the top of Riley's head. He looked back at Penny as he poured two cups of coffee. "You can hardly stand without wincing. You've got two kids to take care of. Why're you fighting my help?"

Why? Because having him here tore at her. Her emotions felt flayed. Being with Colt was too hard. Too nebulous. He was here today but he'd be gone tomorrow and she knew it. The question was, why didn't *he* know it? He was always looking for a way to risk his life. How long would he last in a beach cottage in a sleepy town where the only risk was fighting diaper rash?

"Because you don't belong here, Colt," she said, idly pushing Reid's scattered Cheerios into a pile for him. "I'm not going to count on your 'help' only to watch it disappear."

Shaking his head, he carried both cups of coffee across the room and handed one to her. "I told you. This is different." He waved his cup at the twins. "They make it different."

"For how long?"

"What?"

Her hands curled around the coffee cup, drawing the heat into her palms, sending it rushing through her veins, dispelling the chill she felt. "We were married for a single day before you ended it. You left and never looked back. I won't let you do that to my kids."

"Who says I will?"

"I do," she said, gathering together every last, ragged thread of her remaining self-control. "You live your life with risk, Colt. But I don't. And I won't let my kids live that way, either. Most especially, I won't risk my children's heartbreak on a father who will eventually turn his back and walk away."

"So where is she?"

Late that afternoon, Connor looked around the small living room as if half expecting to find Penny huddled under a throw pillow.

"She's taking a nap," Colt answered and dropped onto the couch. The overstuffed cushions felt so good, he thought he just might stay there for a year or two. "So are the twins."

Connor stuffed his hands into his slacks pockets and rocked back on his heels. "Well, wake 'em up. I want to meet my niece and nephew."

Stunned, Colt stared at his brother for a second. "Are you nuts? This is the first chance I've had to sit down in three hours." His eyes narrowed on his twin. "Wake them up and die."

Connor chuckled, walked to the nearest chair and plopped down into it. "Don't look now, but you sound like a beleaguered housewife."

He frowned at that, then shrugged. "Never again will I say the phrase 'just a housewife.' How the hell do women do it? I've been here two days and I'm beat. Cooking, cleaning, taking care of two babies…" He paused, let his head drop to the couch back and added, "women are made of *way* tougher stuff than us, Con. Trust me."

He stared unseeing up at the beam-and-plaster ceiling overhead and wondered how Penny had coped all alone for the last eight months. Hell, during her pregnancy? A stir of something that felt a lot like regret moved through him and Colt frowned to himself. Yeah, he'd missed a hell of a lot that he would never get back. But she'd been here. On her own, except for her brother—and Robert was an intern so he couldn't have been around much—so how had she done it all?

Okay, yeah, she had been behind on her bills, but the house was clean, the kids were happy and healthy, and she was building her own business. He had to admire that even while it irritated him still that she'd never contacted him. That she refused to need him.

"Was this house built by elves?" Connor muttered.

"I'm getting claustrophobia just sitting here." He glanced up at the ceiling. "Why is that so close?"

Colt sighed. "I almost knocked myself out this morning," he admitted. "I slept on the couch and when the twins cried I jumped up, ran to their room and smacked my forehead on the door frame."

Con held up one finger. "Excuse me? You slept on the couch?"

"Shut up."

"How the mighty have fallen." Con leaned forward, bracing his elbows on his thighs. "Word of this gets out, your rep is shot."

"Word of this gets out," Colt told him, "I'll know who to blame."

"Point taken." Connor leaned back in his chair again with a good-natured shrug. "So, tell me about them. What's it been like?"

Colt laughed and speared one hand through his hair. "Let's see. This morning they dropped my wallet into the toilet, pulled flowers from the pots on the back porch and threw blueberry yogurt onto the kitchen floor just to watch it splat."

Connor grinned. "Sounds normal. And crazy-making."

"You got that right," Colt said on a tired sigh. "How the hell did Penny manage on her own? Not only did she take care of the twins, but she's running a photography business, too. I don't know when she finds the time to pause long enough to take photos of other people's kids when the twins demand constant supervision."

Con laughed outright. "Since when do you start using words like supervision?"

Embarrassed, Colt said, "Since I discovered that climbing Everest is *nothing* compared to giving those two babies a bath. After the yogurt incident, I threw 'em both in the tub and wound up looking like a flood survivor by the end of it."

"And you're loving it?"

Colt's gaze snapped to his twin's. "I didn't say that."

"Didn't have to. Hell, nobody knows you better than I do and I can tell you're enjoying the hell out of this. Even with all the work and yogurt trauma."

A swell of emotion filled Colt as he thought about the twins. The snuffling sounds they made when they were sleeping, the sigh of their breathing, had become a sort of music to him now. He recognized every sound. He knew that Riley wanted to be cuddled before bedtime while Reid wanted to sprawl across his mattress, looking for the most comfortable position.

He knew that Riley loved her brown teddy bear and that Reid preferred a green alligator. He knew Riley wanted Cheerios in the morning and that Reid was interested only in bananas.

His children were real to him now. Actual people— in miniature—with distinct personalities. They had become a part of him and he couldn't have said just when that had happened. But he did know that he wasn't ready for this time with them to end.

"Okay then," Connor interrupted his thoughts abruptly. "You're living in a tiny house, taking care of tiny people and sleeping on a too-short couch. Why?"

"You know why," Colt grumbled and wished for a second he hadn't opened the door to his brother. Didn't he have enough going on at the moment without Con throwing his two cents in?

"Yeah, I do. Now tell me how it's going with Penny."

"Frustrating," Colt admitted, lifting his head to look

at his twin. "She believes she did the right thing in not telling me."

"Did she?"

His eyes narrowed on his brother. "What's that supposed to mean?"

Connor shrugged. "You haven't exactly made a secret of the fact that you don't want a family of your own."

"Whose side are you on, anyway?" Colt sat up straighter.

Lifting both hands for peace, Connor assured him, "Yours. Obviously. But you gotta admit, she had reason to do what she did."

He would have argued, but over the last couple of days, his anger had slowly been drained away until he could think clearly. Logically. And damn it, he could see her point of view. Didn't mean he agreed with it, though. "Fine. She had reason. The point is, I know now and—"

"What're you gonna do about it?"

"That's the thing," Colt muttered. "No idea. You and I both know those kids shouldn't depend on *me*."

"No, I don't know that. For God's sake, Colt, stop beating yourself up." Connor huffed out an impatient breath. "It wasn't your fault. We've all told you that countless times over the last ten years."

"Yeah," he said, staring at his brother. "You all have and it doesn't change a thing. I should've been there. I told them I would be. If I had been…"

Darkness rose up inside him and buzzed in his head like a swarm of attacking bees. Pain jolted him. Memories were thick and for a moment or two, Colt was sure he could actually feel the bite of the snow, taste the cold on the wind. Hear screams that sounded almost nightly in his dreams. He hadn't lived that day, but in his dreams, he did. Over and over again.

"What makes you think you could have stopped it?" Connor jumped up from the chair, stalked across the room and looked down at him. "You weren't responsible. Let it go already."

Colt laughed shortly. *Let it go.* If only it were that easy. But ten years after the darkest day in his life, the memories were still clear and sharp enough to draw blood. How could he forget? How could he ever forgive himself? How could he allow two defenseless infants to depend on *him?*

"You can let it go. I can't." He stood up, meeting his twin's gaze with a steely stare of his own. Didn't matter how close he and Connor were, this was something Colt had to carry on his own. Had to live with. Every. Damn. Day. And no one else would ever understand what it was like to be haunted by thoughts of *what if.*

A couple of tense seconds ticked past as the twins glared at each other. But eventually Connor shrugged, shook his head and said in disgust, "It's amazing you can grow hair on that rock you call a head."

Colt snorted. "This head is identical to yours so choose your insults more wisely."

Connor's lips twitched. "Fine. So let's talk about Sicily instead. You want me to get somebody else to check out Mount Etna for us?"

He'd considered it. There were a couple of experienced climbers they'd used before to scope out new spots when Colt was too busy to do it. But he wasn't ready for that yet. "No," he said, shaking his head firmly. "I'll do it. Might take a week or so until Penny's feeling better, but I'll get to it."

"Your call," Con said, then asked, "So if I'm quiet, can I look at your kids while they sleep?"

Colt gave his brother a quick grin. "Sure. But if you wake 'em up, you'll be here until you put 'em back to sleep."

The rest of the afternoon passed on a tide of diapers, baby food, Cheerios and crazed babies crawling all over the house—usually in two separate directions. Colt was too busy to do a lot of thinking. But he still managed to have an idea that kept swimming through his mind, refusing to be ignored. He played with possibilities as he bathed the twins and then wrestled them into pajamas. Not easy since Reid refused to lie still and Riley insisted on tearing her diaper off the minute Colt got it on her.

How in the hell had his life changed so completely, so quickly?

Colt was getting into a routine and the fact that he could actually *think* that word and not run screaming for the closest exit was almost scary. But routines were meant to be broken. This wasn't forever.

But as he looked at the babies now settling into their cribs for the night, he realized that knowing this time was going to end didn't make him as happy as it should have. He scrubbed one hand across the back of his neck and tried to sort through the splintered thoughts and emotions raging inside him.

The twins had laid siege to his heart, there was no denying it. What he felt when he looked at them, when they smiled up at him or threw their little arms around his neck, was indescribable. Sure, he'd been around his cousins and heard them all talking about how their children had affected them. But he guessed you couldn't really *understand* until you'd experienced it for yourself.

Two tiny children—not even talking yet—and they'd

changed everything for him. He just didn't know what to do to protect them, other than to keep his distance.

Problem was, he wasn't ready to leave just yet.

"Enjoying your special time with the twins?"

The voice from the doorway behind him didn't surprise him. In spite of the turmoil in his mind, Colt had *felt* Penny there watching him long before she spoke.

Glancing over his shoulder at her he said, "I don't know how you take care of them so well on your own."

She looked surprised by the compliment and a quick stab of guilt hit him. Colt realized that in the last few days he had never acknowledged just what she'd accomplished in this tiny house. She'd been on her own from the jump, yet she'd managed to care for the twins and this house and try to build a business.

Exhausted him just thinking about what her life must have been like for the last eight months.

"Well, thanks." She stiffened a little as if she'd been unprepared for flattery—and didn't quite know how to take it. She fidgeted with the short, pale blue robe she was wearing, tugging the terry cloth lapels tighter across her chest. "It isn't always easy, but—"

"Oh, I get that." He stared down at his daughter, lying in her crib. In her favorite position, with her behind pointed at the sky, the tiny girl smiled as she drifted off to sleep. Shaking his head in amazement, Colt looked over at Reid, who was already sleeping, sprawled across the mattress as if trying to claim every inch of the space as his own.

Twins, but so different. Yet both of them had carved their essences into his heart in a matter of days. It was damn humbling for a man who was used to running the world around him to admit, even to himself, that two tiny babies could bring him to his knees.

Walking to the doorway, Colt turned out the light and watched as the night-light tossed softly glowing stars onto the ceiling. Then he and Penny stepped into the hallway and he pulled the door closed behind them.

In the sudden silence, he stared down at her and lost himself for a second in the deep green of her eyes. The whole world was quiet and the tension between them flashed hot as she gathered the neck of her robe in one fist. His body went to stone when he realized she was *naked* under that robe.

And in a heartbeat, his memory provided him with a very clear image of her naked body. The curves he'd spent hours exploring. The smooth slide of his hand across her skin. The fullness of her breasts, the slick heat of her body surrounding his.

His eyes narrowed on the top of her robe, as if just by concentrating, he could make her release that death grip and give him a peek at what lay beneath. Damn, the woman was going to kill him.

"I'm, uh, going to take a shower," she said and took a step back from him.

Colt's eyes narrowed on her. "Are you steady enough to do it on your own?"

Her eyes went wide at the implication that if she wasn't, he was going to help.

"I'm fine," she insisted, taking another step backward. He could have told her that a few feet of distance wouldn't be enough to put out the flames snapping between them.

Then she was talking again, her words coming quickly, almost breathlessly, as she tried to make her escape. "I'm tired of washing up. And they said I could take a shower sooner than this, I was just nervous about it. So now I'm not and I really want a shower."

Hot water, sluicing across her body, cascading over smooth skin, soap bubbles sliding down the length of her amazing legs. Colt cursed silently. If he kept up this train of thought, he wouldn't be able to walk. He wanted her badly, but he was also worried. What if she got into the shower and needed help?

His inner cynic snorted at that one. He wanted to be in that shower with her, but it wasn't *help* he wanted to give her.

"It's not safe for you to be in there on your own," he said, a part of him actually believing the statement. "I'll help you."

"Oh, no." She shook her head hard enough for her long, dark red hair to swing out from her shoulders. "Not gonna happen."

"Don't argue." He took her arm and steered her down the short hall to the bathroom. "We're adults, Penny."

"Yeah," she murmured, "that's the problem."

He gave her a wicked wink. "Are you saying you can't trust yourself around me? Can't control your raging desire to rip off my clothes and take me? Take me hard?"

Her lips twitched and he grinned back at her.

"That's exactly right, Colt," she said, sarcasm dripping from every word. "I don't want to take advantage of you in your weakened state."

"Very thoughtful," he assured her and walked into the bathroom, also designed for people a foot shorter than Colt, keeping a firm grip on her elbow. "Look, seriously, you need a shower and I'm not going to let you risk falling or something."

"What am I, ninety? I'm not going to fall. I'm not an invalid," she told him as he turned on the water and waited impatiently for it to heat up.

He let go of her, but blocked the only exit so she couldn't sidle out of the room. "All kidding aside," he said, "you can argue and we can be here for hours, or we can just get this taken care of."

She thought about that for a long minute or two, the pitiful sound of the low-water-pressure shower in the background. "Fine. You can stay in the room, but no looking."

He snorted. "I'll try to control myself."

And it would be an effort, he thought but didn't say. The room was so small, they were practically standing in the same space. The short, narrow sink dug into his thigh as he moved aside to let her get to the shower.

"Turn around," she ordered.

He did and found himself staring into the mirror—something she clearly hadn't considered. Behind him, she was reflected in the glass as she slipped out of her robe. He gritted his teeth as his gaze followed the line of her spine right down to the curve of her truly amazing behind. Her hair danced across the top of her back as she moved and he wanted to tangle his hands in that thick, soft mass as he had before.

His body throbbing, aching, Colt held his ground, though it cost him every last ounce of his self-control. Never before had he been forced to *not* take what he wanted. To stand back and let the woman driving him insane slip through his fingers. His teeth ground together and his breath came short and fast. Still, he couldn't look away and was rewarded—or tortured—with a glimpse of her breasts, high and full, as she pulled the striped curtain back and stepped into the tub.

The water ran and he heard her blissful sigh and that was nearly enough to push him over the edge. Colt looked at the curtain and imagined her behind it, naked and wet, tipping her face up to the stingy flow of water. He couldn't help wondering what she would think of the shower at his place, with its six massaging heads and the heated seats carved into the granite enclosure. In his mind, he laid her down on that wide seat, parted her thighs and—

"Ow."

"What?" he snapped, dream dissolving instantly. "What is it?"

"Nothing," she said. "I just moved too fast and I'm still a little sore, that's all. I'm fine."

He didn't believe her. If she pulled her stitches out, they'd be back to square one.

Pulling the curtain aside, he looked at her and instantly knew it had been a mistake. His imagination had *nothing* on the reality of a slick, wet, naked Penny. Her long, dark red hair hung in thick ropes over her shoulders. Drops of water clung to the tips of her hardened nipples and her face was flush with warmth and surprise. She looked like a damn water nymph and his body's reaction was instantaneous.

The tiny window over the shower was open, allowing a cold breeze to whisper through. The sea-green paint was peeling on the ceiling and the porcelain on the ancient tub was scratched and pitted. Yet all he gave a damn about was the wet, naked woman looking at him with raw desire in her eyes.

She shook her head and chewed at her bottom lip before saying, "Go away, Colt."

"No," he said, unable to tear his gaze from her. There was no way he was leaving. If it had meant his life, he still would have stayed exactly where he was.

Raw, frantic lust pumped hot through him. Desire clutched at his throat, making breathing nearly impossible. But then, he asked himself as he reached out one hand to cup her breast, *who needed to breathe?*

She gasped at his touch, and rather than moving back, she stepped closer and licked her lips, sending a lightning bolt of need slicing through him. Then she covered his hand with hers, holding him steady against her breast. Struggling for air, she whispered brokenly, "We can't. We shouldn't. I mean, I shouldn't. I mean—"

He knew what she meant. She'd had surgery a few days before. Everything between them was a mess, with neither of them happy with the other at the moment. And yet… "We'll be careful…."

"Colt—" she gasped again as his thumb caressed her hardened nipple. "Oh, my."

He smiled to himself, then stepped back long enough to shed his clothes and toe off his shoes. Then he was joining her in the made-for-munchkins shower.

Suddenly, he was liking the small space. She couldn't have backed away from him even if she had wanted to. And one look into her eyes told him she didn't want to.

"This is so not a good idea," she whispered.

"Stop thinking," he said.

Seven

Then he kissed her.

As the trickle of water splashed over their entwined bodies, he kissed her long and deep, losing himself in the taste and feel of her. When she parted her lips under his, he took the kiss deeper, tangling his tongue with hers in a frenzied dance of need and want. *Here it is,* he thought wildly. That amazing jolt of passion that he'd never felt for anyone else. The elemental, nearly primitive need to touch and take and have.

Only with her. Only with Penny.

She wrapped her arms around his neck and leaned into him, her breasts sliding against his chest. He ran his hands up and down her body, the slick feel of her skin beneath his hands a match held to the dynamite crouched inside him. "Damn, you feel good."

"You, too," she whispered. "Blast it, you, too."

He smiled against her mouth. She didn't *want* to want him, he thought. But she did and that was good enough. Colt turned her so that her back was to the water tumbling from the narrow, outdated showerhead. She looked up at him as the hot water landed on her shoulders to roll down her body in rivulets.

"Colt—"

"Let me touch you," he whispered, sliding one hand down from her breast. His fingertips trailed along her rib cage and down over her abdomen.

She shivered, closed her eyes and hissed in a breath. "I don't know…"

"I do," he said and kissed her again as he dipped first one finger and then two into her tight, wet heat.

She gasped and clutched at him, hands grabbing at his shoulders. Her breath came fast and shallow, small puffs against his skin. He touched her deeper, stroking her intimately until she rocked into his hand, reaching for the climax he was pushing her toward. His thumb moved over the heart of her, that one nub of sensation that fueled the fire inside her until it became a raging inferno.

She spread her legs for him, welcoming his touch, his caresses. Then she slid one hand from his shoulders, down the length of his body until her long, delicate fingers closed around the hard length of him. Then it was Colt's turn to hiss in air and tremble under the onslaught of too many sensations.

"That's cheating," he said softly.

"All's fair—you know." She groaned as he stroked her again, rubbing the core of her harder while his fingers delved deeper inside her body.

He took her—and she took him. Her fingers moved on him until it was all Colt could do to keep his feet. His vision blurred as completion roared toward him. But he wouldn't do it. Wouldn't surrender to what she was making him feel. Not until he'd seen her shatter in his arms.

It didn't take much longer.

He kissed her hungrily, allowing her to feel everything he felt. He wanted her to know what she was doing to him. Her breath quickened. She tore her mouth from his. Her eyes went wide and wild and she shouted his name hoarsely as her climax slammed into her.

Colt held her close until the last of her tremors had passed. Only then did he think about himself and the fact that his body was aching for the same release she'd just experienced. Then Penny looked up into his eyes and smiled. Her grasp on him tightened and he surged into her hand. Her thumb moved over the tip of him and that sensation nearly sent him over the edge. His self-control was unraveling. Fast.

No other woman had ever affected him like Penny could. From the first moment he'd met her, there had been an electricity between them. A single touch was all it took to shower them both with sparks that they could find nowhere else. Everything about her was…more. She excited him, infuriated him and aroused him more than he would have believed possible.

But when he came, it was going to be *inside her.* He pulled away from her only long enough that she was forced to stop rubbing and stroking him, though the action cost him. Aching need clawed at him and he read new desire in Penny's eyes, too. They had always been explosive when they came together and it seemed nothing had changed since he'd last seen her.

"That's it," he muttered. "Bed. We need the bed."

"But we shouldn't—" Her mouth might be saying no but her eyes were shouting *yes*.

"Is it safe for you to have sex?" he muttered thickly, saying a silent prayer that she would say yes again.

"They said as soon as I felt ready."

"Please tell me you're ready."

"Boy howdy."

He grinned at her quick response. Dropping his forehead to hers, he muttered, "We'll be careful. You can be on top. You set the pace. That's my best offer."

"I'll take it." She swallowed hard, reached behind her to turn off the water, then allowed Colt to pick her up and carry her out of the bathroom and into her room.

The bed was narrow, but Colt didn't care. All he wanted was a damn flat surface. He flopped onto the mattress and watched as she climbed up to cover his body with hers.

She was so small-boned. So delicate. So damn sexy.

"Wait," he ground out. "Condom."

"Yeah, because it worked so well before," she said wryly.

He snorted. "Good point."

"Doesn't matter," she told him. "I'm covered."

"Best news I've heard all night." He lay back again and clamped his hands onto her hips.

As she went up onto her knees, he took a breath and held it. She looked like some warrior princess from ancient tales of Ireland. Her dark red hair streamed wetly across her shoulders to lay across the tops of her breasts. Her green eyes flashed with intent and her pale skin shone like the finest porcelain. She was damned magnificent and he wanted her more than his next breath.

* * *

Penny trembled from head to foot. This was a bad idea and she knew it. But there was no way she could stop now. She had to have Colton King inside her again. She needed to feel the thick, hard length of him filling her body completely. She'd worry about tomorrow when it reared its ugly head. For right now, she was going to live in the moment. This one, amazing, incredible moment— she was going to take everything she could from it.

"You just going to torture us all night?" he asked, his voice a low, throaty growl of contained passion.

"That's the plan," she murmured, gaze locked on his as she slowly lowered herself onto him, taking him into her body inch by glorious inch. Penny watched his ice-blue eyes flash with heat and the last lingering whisper of reason in her mind faded away.

She knew this was stupid. She knew nothing had changed. Colt still wouldn't stay. They had no future. But for this one perfect moment in time she was going to forget all of that.

She'd wanted him, needed him, *missed* him and now he was here. In her bed, looking at her as if she were the only woman in the world. Desire quickened, her breath came faster and feverish bubbles of expectation rose inside her. She moved on him, felt him catch her rhythm and move with her and she surrendered to the inevitable.

Colt King was the only man she would ever want. Damn it, the only man she would ever *love* and this might be all she ever had of him. How could she possibly deny herself what she found only with him?

She took him deep and when he was fully sheathed inside her, she sighed a little as her body stretched to accommodate his. Excitement rippled through her sys-

tem, lighting fires that had been simmering for nearly
two years. What she'd had with Colt would never truly
be extinguished. One touch from him and those flames
had erupted and consumed her in an inferno of sensations. It had been like this between them from the start.

They fit so well together it was as if they had been
meant to find each other.

She rocked her body on his and heard his swift in-
take of breath. Penny trailed her fingers across his chest
and down, loving the feel of his hard, muscular body beneath her hands. Dark hair dusted his chest and trailed
down his abdomen. The muscles in his arms flexed as
he reached up to cup her breasts in his palms. Sighing
with the intense pleasure soaring inside her, she tipped
her head back and gasped as his thumbs slid back and
forth across her hardened nipples.

Penny's head tipped back and she felt the cool slap of
her still-damp hair against her skin. He touched her and
she spun out of control. He moved inside her and she
only wanted more.

Her body ached a little as she moved on him, but that
tiny pain was lost in a dizzying parade of feelings that
had nothing to do with discomfort.

Darkness crouched outside the window and a soft
wind rattled the tree limbs against the side of the house.
Inside, though, it was all heat and magic and straining
breathing and racing hearts.

Penny felt the lost time without him in her life melt
away until only this one moment existed. The passion
she remembered roared up stronger, sharper, more overpowering than before and she gave herself up to it. Staring down into his eyes, she moved on him, loving the
feel of him sliding in and out of her body. He filled her

so completely, the slightest movement created a friction that left her breathless. Again and again she moved on him, setting the pace, watching his eyes flare with heat and desire. Her blood pumped fast and furious, until it became a roaring in her ears, shutting out every other sound. An exquisite, oh so familiar tingle of expectation began to build deep inside her.

Colt's hands moved over her body, touching, exploring, tantalizing her with more and more sensations. He moved beneath her, picking up the rhythm she set and meeting her at every stroke, pushing them both faster and higher.

She groaned, braced her hands on his broad, muscled chest and raced to meet the climax that was hovering just out of reach. She climbed the peak in front of her quickly, desperate to reach the top and then tumble off the other side.

"Come for me, Penny," he whispered and his voice was a caress on every raw nerve ending. "Come for me. Let me watch you fly."

Throat tight, air strangling in her lungs, she was almost there, her body alive and simmering with want. Need. Her eyes flew open, locked with his, and when the first tremor shuddered inside her, she raced to meet it.

Colt shifted one hand to where their bodies were joined. His thumb caressed that one spectacular spot and as he watched, Penny shattered into a million jagged pieces.

Her mind was still spinning, her body still buzzing when she felt his body explode into hers. She heard his guttural shout, felt the tension in him coil and then release as, locked together, they crashed into oblivion.

* * *

A short while later, Colt rolled out of the cramped bed, pulled on his jeans and left her sleeping, curled on her side. He stared down at her, his gaze tracking the curves of her naked body, and hunger grabbed him by the throat again. She was beautiful. And amazing. And *dangerous*.

He laid the faded, flowered quilt over her, then slipped out of the room. The house was quiet. Too damn quiet, if truth be told. He wasn't used to this. The world he lived in was noisy, crowded and rushed—a place where no one got too close and he could move through crowds of people without ever being touched by any of them.

It's the way he liked it, he assured himself, as he quietly checked on the twins, then moved through the darkened house like a caged tiger looking for the easiest escape. He found it as he walked through the kitchen, opening the back door and stepping into the smartphone-size backyard.

He pulled in a deep breath of the cool night air and held it inside, hoping that it might swamp the fires still raging within. Naturally, it didn't, and he was left to burn as he took a seat on the steps and stared up at the sky.

Colt was still trying to come to grips with what had just happened. Being with Penny had rocked him right down to his bones. He was used to desire. Used to slaking that desire with whatever woman was handy. What he wasn't used to was what happened to him with Penny.

Over the last couple of years, he'd convinced himself that the memories he carried of his week with Penny were exaggerated. That no one could be that amazing. That the…connection he felt with her didn't really exist. Well, those lies had just been smashed.

His heart felt like a jackhammer in his chest and his

mind was filled with a jumble of thoughts he couldn't sort through.

Sex with Penny was staggering. No other way to put it or think of it.

Stars spilled across the blackness and a quarter moon looked like a child's teeter-totter. *Child.* The twins' features swam into his mind and he felt himself tighten up. Thoughts of sex dissolved as he considered the reason he was here. Those two kids deserved better than this cramped, too-short-for-real-people house. They were *Kings*. He could admire Penny for all she'd accomplished on her own, but now that he was in the picture, things were going to change.

He was putting his own life and business on hold to be here for Penny and the twins, but that couldn't last. He had places he had to be—Mount Etna, to be specific.

That thought quickly spiraled into another and from there, his brain raced with ideas. A slow smile spread across his face as he considered one notion in particular. Hell, he could go to Etna this week. And Penny and the kids could go to Sicily with him. The twins could see some of the world—never too young to experience different things. Then Penny could take photos of his BASE jumps to be used in advertising and that would help her business.

Smiling to himself, he nodded thoughtfully as the plan came together.

"You must be out of your mind entirely." Penny stared at him the next morning, astonished at what he'd just said.

Colt spooned more yogurt into two waiting mouths and flicked her a glance. "Not at all. This is perfect. I get my work done, you get some advertising for your business and the kids get to fly on a private jet. A win all the way around."

Shaking her head, Penny grabbed her cup of coffee and took a long drink, hoping that caffeine would give her the strength to deal with Colt. She'd awakened that morning alone in her bed, and though she was disappointed, she hadn't been surprised. Colt wasn't the snuggling kind of man and she knew it. And still there was a flicker of pain when she was forced to acknowledge that he was keeping a distance between them—even after what they'd shared.

But *this* was nuts.

"You can't really expect us to go to Sicily with you."

"Why not?" He shrugged, wiped Riley's mouth with a paper towel, then shoveled more yogurt into her. "We'll give it another week. You should be good to go by then."

Was it really so easy for him? Just make a decision and go? She had responsibilities. The twins to think of. A business to build. A house to take care of. Which she told him.

"The house will be fine. The twins will be with us," he looked at her again. "As for your business, it's at a standstill and you know it. I looked into your files this morning while you were sleeping. You're barely covering expenses."

Outrage and embarrassment tangled inside her, convulsing into tight knots that felt like balls of ice in the pit of her stomach. Not only had he delved into her bank account and her bills, he'd snooped through her business. He'd riffled through her records and all he'd seen was the bottom line. He hadn't noticed the hard work, the hopes, the dreams.

"I can't believe you did that," she murmured, then

laughed shortly at her own naïveté. Of course he'd intruded. Of course he'd stuck his nose into her business. Look what he'd done to her *life!*

The night before, she'd allowed herself to forget just how wide a gulf separated them. She'd indulged her senses and put her logical self on the back burner. But now Sensible Penny was back in charge.

Keeping her voice light so the twins wouldn't pick up on any tension, she focused a laser glare on Colt. "My business isn't any of yours."

"Wrong," he said easily. Then before she could argue, he continued. "I'm not looking for a battle here, Penny. I'm just saying, your business could use a good boost— and taking pictures for King's Extreme Adventures would give you that."

She slumped back in her kitchen chair. Sunlight fell through the windows and lay across the table and the old oak flooring. "Yes, because nothing says 'I'll take great pictures of your toddler' like doing a photo spread of an insane man jumping off a volcano."

A wry grin touched his mouth briefly and she felt the punch of it to her middle. But she wouldn't be seduced again.

"Colt, I didn't ask for your help and I don't need it."

"That's a matter of opinion."

"But mine is the only one I'm concerned with."

He sprinkled a few Cheerios onto the twins' tray tables and finally turned to meet her gaze squarely. "I'm offering you a job. It pays well. And," he added with a slow smile, "there are *other* benefits."

That swirl of something hot and wicked punched her low again and even melted a couple of the ice knots. But enough of them remained to keep her on course.

"We are *not* taking the babies on an excursion to a volcano. And no," she added, "I don't want to take pictures of you risking your safety, much less have my children witness that. Do you want them scarred for life?"

He snorted. "I don't remember you being so squeamish. When we met you were into sports photography. You wanted to travel the world, capturing danger and excitement with your camera." Shaking his head, he looked at her quizzically. "Now you're happy to take pictures of suburbia? What happened to all of the big dreams?"

"I became a mom," she said, trying to make him understand, though she doubted he ever would. "Plans change. *Dreams* change."

Her words were soft but powerful, and he acknowledged that with a brief nod for her. Then Colt looked at the twins and she watched his features soften and his eyes warm. She knew that his children had reached him in a way she'd never been able to. But she also knew that this time in her cottage was a blip on his radar screen. It didn't matter how much he cared for the twins.

Colton King, as he'd told her himself, was not the staying kind.

Friday morning, Rafe King from King Construction was at Penny's house bright and early. Colt was glad for the distraction. Since his brilliant plan had been shot down the day before by Penny, the two of them had been staying out of each other's way. Which wasn't easy in a house no bigger than a good-sized garden shed.

Carrying two cups of coffee with him, Colt strode out of the house and met his cousin as he climbed down from his truck.

"Coffee." Rafe grinned as he reached for it. "You always were my favorite cousin."

"And your wife's my favorite cousin-in-law." Colt looked past Rafe into the cab of the truck. "Did Katie take pity on me and send cookies?"

Rafe's wife, widely known as "Katie King the Cookie Queen," ran her own business out of her home while taking care of their daughter, Becca, and their newborn son, Braden. She also baked cookies for the legions of King cousins who adored her.

"Nice to see you, too," Rafe said wryly. After taking a sip of coffee, he reached into the truck and came back out with a white bakery box stamped "Cookie Queen."

Colt made a grab for it but Rafe whipped it out of reach. "Not for you," he said, and seemed to enjoy the moment. "Katie sent these to Penny. Along with her commiseration on being involved with a King."

Scowling, Colt pointed out, "Doesn't say much for you, does it?"

"Nah," Rafe said with a grin and a shrug. "She *likes* me."

"Great." His gaze locked on the pastry box. "What kind?"

"White chocolate macadamia."

"That's just mean," Colt said.

"My wife's good."

"That she is." Colt looked at Rafe and thought about it. Not that long ago, Rafe had been as determinedly single as Colt was and yet now he was happily married to a great woman and had two kids. He thought about taking a step back just in case commitment was contagious. On the other hand, he was already hip-deep in familyland, wasn't he?

"How's Katie and the new baby?"

Rafe's grin got wider. "Amazing. He's gorgeous and Katie's…even better than amazing. We're gonna have a big party for the christening. You and Con'll be there, right?"

"Absolutely." Colt had been to more christenings in the last few years than he had in all the years before. But every King birth was celebrated. Every new member to the family had to be welcomed with a barbecue and lots of food and laughs.

Which reminded him, he should talk to Penny about introducing the twins to the rest of the Kings. Not that they could have a King-size party at the cottage. They'd never be able to shoehorn everyone in. But they could hold it at his place. God knew there was plenty of room.

Funny, he'd never realized before that the house he bought three years ago was really meant for a big family. He'd thought at the time that it was a good investment. It still was, of course, but now he had to wonder how Penny and the twins would like it there. It would be better for them, he thought. More room. Big yard. Close to the beach.

He gave his head a hard shake. Seriously, he was beginning to worry about himself.

Rafe asked suddenly, "So, how's your new baby? Wait a minute. *Babies*."

"Not exactly new," Colt said. "They're eight months old."

"Right." Rafe leaned against the truck. "Con told me. That couldn't have been easy."

"No, it wasn't." And it wasn't getting any easier, either.

He was feeling nothing but conflicted about this whole situation. He wanted those kids happy and safe. But to keep them that way, he knew that he couldn't stick around. He couldn't be here, let them learn to count on him only to risk letting them down when they most needed him. The thought of not being there to hear their first words or to watch them learning to walk tore at him. The thought of never seeing Penny again hit him much harder than he wanted to admit.

But there was no place for him here in this tiny house with a family. Because to stay would mean that they would come to depend on him. And he would, eventually, let them down. Hell, that's the one thing he could agree with Penny on. She was worried that he would disappoint his children—and so was he.

"How you doin' with all of it?"

"I'm all right." And not interested in talking about this. Even with a cousin. "Really appreciate you moving on the roof this fast."

"Not a problem. Anything for a King." Rafe shot a look at the roof on Penny's cottage and frowned. "That roof's in sad shape."

Hell, most of the house was in sad shape. He knew Penny loved it, but he had to wonder if the real reason she was living there was because it didn't cost her anything. The rooms were too small and the twins were going to outgrow it soon. There was no room for them to play and with only one bathroom, things were going to get ugly at some point.

And *why* was he suddenly thinking about things like that? When did he ever do future planning or worry about yard size or whether a roof was going to make it through another winter? What the hell was happening to him?

Scowling to himself, he muttered, "Check for termites too, will ya? I've got a feeling this place is a buffet lunch for the damn things."

"Okay, I'll get the ladder off the truck, do an inspection, then come find you."

"Like I said, I appreciate this." Colt took another sip of his coffee and tried to put aside the disturbing Suburban Dad thoughts.

Rafe grinned. "What's family for?" He handed over the box of cookies. "Here. Take these in to Penny. I'll see you both in a bit."

"Okay. How soon can you get started on the work?"

"Typical King," Rafe mused. "Why were we all born impatient?"

"Just lucky, I guess." Colt shrugged.

Nodding, Rafe said, "Let me take a look and some measurements. Check for termite damage. Once we've got that I can lay out the plan for you. But I can have a crew here by Monday if that's what you want."

"The quicker the better." He couldn't leave until he knew that Penny and the kids were going to be safe and as comfortable in this tiny dollhouse as it was possible to be. And he knew that with Rafe and his brothers' company on the job, the work would not only be done fast, but well.

With King Construction handling the work, he could assure Penny everything would be taken care of the right way. As for Rafe—he and his brothers ran such a successful construction and contracting business that they seldom had to go out on calls themselves. But the Kings were always there for family, so it didn't surprise Colt at all that Rafe had shown up personally.

So, if the Kings were always there for family and he was planning on getting out of his kids' lives as fast as possible, just what kind of King did that make him?

Eight

Of course there were termites.

And not just a few, either. No, this was a regular condo association of termites. They had community leaders, Miss California Termite pageants and apparently, never-ending appetites for the wood holding up her roof.

Penny sighed and grabbed Riley before the baby could crawl off the quilt spread on the lawn in the backyard. Reid was busily tearing apart one of his books, but Riley wasn't as easily contained. Absently, Penny handed her daughter a busy box and then looked up at the men on her roof. Rafe was a sweetie and yes, it was…nice of Colt to arrange all of this.

But at the heart of everything, Penny just kept sinking deeper and deeper into the "I owe Colton King" hole. But the worst part was, she wasn't even angry about owing him. She was just too relieved to have some of the bigger worries in her life smoothed over. So what did that make her? A hypocrite?

She accused Colt of using his money to make his own path easier. She was outraged when he interfered and paid off her credit cards just before dropping a fortune into her bank account. And she'd been furious about him arranging for a new roof. Or at least, that's how she'd acted. But the truth was, she was grateful and she hated to admit that.

She was both relieved and resentful—not exactly rational. But then she'd never been completely rational when it came to Colton King. Besides, putting her own confusing feelings aside, she knew Colt well enough to know exactly why he was doing all of this. He was taking care of everything he thought needed doing so that he could disappear with a clear conscience.

Penny took a deep breath and tried to steady herself as a wave of disappointment and dread washed through her. Two nights ago, she and Colt had come together and the passion had been staggering. What was between them was so strong, so overpowering, that even remembering what they'd shared shook her right to the bone.

But neither of them had so much as talked about it. She could almost believe it hadn't happened at all. Except for the fact that her body was in a constant state of low burn from a fire that had been reignited. Being with Colt again had not only reawakened her body, but her dreams. Nearly two years ago, when they'd first met, Penny had fallen in love so quickly, so completely, she had looked at their shared future and seen only the magic and the joy. Soon enough, reality had crashed down on her, leaving her brokenhearted and alone. It hadn't been easy to recover, to move on. And now, she knew instinctively that this time, recovery was going to be so much harder.

She'd known, of course, that she still loved Colt. Love just wasn't something that ended. At least, not for Penny. And being here with him, seeing him with the twins, had only etched him deeper into her heart than he had been before. Which was, she knew, a recipe for disaster.

She could already feel him pulling away from her. From the twins. It was as if the closer to being healed Penny became, the faster Colt was drawing back. She only wished it was that easy to turn down her feelings for him. The sad truth was, she still loved him. She'd never *stopped* loving him. But at least until this week, she'd taught herself to live without him in her life.

Now he was back and it was harder than ever to imagine going on without him. Her heart ached with the might-have-beens that rotated through her brain at all hours of the day and night. She looked at her babies and felt desolate that their father would be only a visitor in their lives. They would miss out on so much—and so would Colt. He didn't even realize it, but in leaving, he was cheating himself. She knew he didn't see it that way, though. There was something driving Colt. He was a warm, funny, intelligent man who was determined to live his life alone. Why? What was it in his past that kept him from seeing a chance at a future?

Reid turned his face up to hers at just that moment. A sweet smile curved his little mouth; his blue eyes were shining with love and trust and sheer joy. His soft black hair blew across his forehead and his chubby hands lifted his book to his mouth. Penny's aching heart melted a little and she wished suddenly that Colt could see just what he was running from. That he would discover the truth in time. But she wasn't holding her breath.

Her gaze shifted to the roofline, where one of Rafe's crews was working diligently. Colt had been up there, too, until about an hour ago. It was in his nature to take risks, even if it was only walking along a roofline as if he were on a tightrope. He was so busy keeping busy that he couldn't see what was right in front of him. The biggest adrenaline rush in the world. Love.

"Oh, this isn't good, is it?"

Penny jerked out of her daydreams and shifted her gaze to Maria as she picked her way across the yard. She wore a black skirt and a red blazer over a white silk blouse, and her three-inch heels kept sinking into the grass as she walked.

"Hi. What did you say?"

"I said, this doesn't look good." She squinted up at the crew on the roof, getting ready to spread a striped tent over the house. "Termites?"

"Only a few bazillion."

Maria shook her head and said, "If they're tenting, why're you still here? Shouldn't you be at Colt's place?"

"We will be, this afternoon," Penny said on a sigh. She wasn't looking forward to it, but she didn't have much choice, either. At the moment, Colt had a team of people inside the cottage, preparing for the termite extermination. But once the tent was up and the gas pumped in, she and the kids wouldn't be able to get back inside for at least forty-eight hours. Which meant either she try to keep the twins happy locked up in a motel room…or, she did what Colt was insisting on. Move in at his place for the duration.

It was hard enough having him here at her house.

What was it going to be like staying with him? Heck, she'd never even seen the place Colt called home. Was it a palace? A condo? A plush penthouse apartment? He hadn't eased her curiosity, either, he'd just said, "You'll see when we get there."

"You sound thrilled at the prospect," Maria said, stepping out of her heels to take a seat on the blanket. Automatically, she swept Reid up onto her lap where the baby boy chortled happily and busied himself with the gold chain Maria wore around her neck.

"Well, it's weird," Penny tried to explain. "Moving into his house is completely different than having him here."

Maria nodded sagely. "The home turf advantage you mean."

"Exactly!" Penny smiled, pulled blades of grass from Riley's hand and added, "I don't want to owe him any more, you know?"

"I'm sorry," Maria said, shaking her head. "I must have gone momentarily deaf. *You* owe *him?* You already gave him two kids. How much more could the bill be?"

Penny laughed in spite of the situation. Maria was not only Robert's fiancée, but a really good friend. And right now, Penny needed one. "Maria, he paid off my bills. He stuck his nose in and used his money to 'straighten out my life.'"

"Good for him."

"What? Aren't you on my side?"

"Absolutely. But why shouldn't he pay off your bills? Honestly, Penny, pride's a great thing. But I'd rather have electricity than sit in the dark telling myself over and over again how proud I am."

"Some help you are."

"Hey, I'm a lawyer. We're soulless, remember?"

Penny laughed again. "I keep forgetting that part. And how did you know I'd be here?"

"Colt told me."

"Told you? When did you see him?"

Maria pulled the gold chain out of Reid's mouth and said, "At the hospital. I was supposed to meet Robert for lunch today but when I got there, he and Colt were just heading to the cafeteria."

"What? Why?" Colt went to see her brother? Without bothering to mention it to her? What was going on? What was he up to now? There was just no telling. Nothing was sacred to Colt. He'd invaded every aspect of her life and there was no sign of his stopping.

Maria shrugged, and kissed the top of Reid's head. "I don't know. Rob just said he'd see me at home later. But they looked…serious."

"Great." Now she could worry about what her brother and her— Wait. Just what *was* Colt to her? Her ex? Sure, but there was more. Her baby daddy? Yep, that, too. Her lover? Everything inside her curled up into a ball and whimpered at the thought. One night with Colt had her dreaming of *more* nights with Colt and that was just piling mistakes on mistakes and she knew it.

Didn't stop the wanting, though. Didn't stop the wishing or the misery that accompanied the knowledge that wishes very rarely came true.

"God. You're still in love with him, aren't you?"

Penny's gaze snapped to Maria's and she felt a flush fill her cheeks. "Of course not. That would be completely stupid."

Maria lifted one eyebrow and gave Penny her best lawyer glare.

"Okay, fine. Yes, you're right." Penny pulled the hem of her T-shirt from Riley's mouth. "I still love him since apparently I don't learn from my own mistakes."

"And what're you going to do about it?"

"Suffer," Penny muttered. "I'm going to watch him walk away. Again. And then I'm going to ask Robert if they've got an anti-love virus inoculation."

Maria laughed. "Pitiful. Really."

"Easy for you to say," Penny whispered. "Robert's crazy about you."

"I know." Maria sighed happily. "I really love that about him. But as for you—why are you so willing to let him walk away again?"

"What am I supposed to do?" Penny asked. "Tie him to the bed?"

"Not an entirely bad idea."

"True. But eventually, he'd work his way free and then he'd leave anyway." She plucked a rock from Riley's fingers and tossed it into the closest flower bed. "Besides, if he's that anxious to get away from me and his children, why should I try to make him stay?"

"Love."

"One-sided love? Not a good time."

"You could fight for him," Maria suggested.

"No." Shaking her head, Penny said, "What would be the point? If I fight and lose, none of it mattered."

"And if you fight and win?"

"I still lose," Penny told her solemnly. "It's no use, Maria. Colt lives for risk. He likes the rush. He likes the danger. I have a feeling that he's not going to be satisfied until he's cheated death so often that he finally catches up to it." She shivered at the thought, then looked at her babies and shook her head again. "I won't watch him do that, Maria. I won't watch him chase death. I can't. And I won't let my kids watch it, either."

A Spanish language radio station blared music into the quiet neighborhood. The men on the roof spreading a green-striped tarp shouted to one another and laughed while they worked.

"So that's it?" Maria watched her. "It's just over now?"

Penny smoothed her palm over Riley's head, loving the feel of her soft curls. "No. It's not over *now*. It was over almost two years ago. It was over right after it began."

The hospital cafeteria wasn't exactly filled with ambiance. But they'd done what they could with the place. Dozens of tables and chairs dotted the gleaming linoleum floor. Windows on the walls allowed bright shafts of daylight into the room and there was a patio through a set of French doors that boasted dappled shade and neatly tended flower beds.

Still, not a place Colt would have chosen to have a lunch meeting. But when you were meeting a busy doctor with limited time, it served its purpose.

Colt looked at the man opposite him. "You did the right thing telling me about the twins."

Robert took a bite of his chicken sandwich, chewed and said, "You had a right to know. But more importantly," he added, waving his sandwich for emphasis, "Penny's been struggling long enough on her own."

"Yeah, she has." Irritation swelled. Remembering what he'd discovered when he went through her bills, her business records, Colt felt another sharp stab of guilt. Though why the hell he should feel guilty, he didn't know. He hadn't *known* about the twins, had he? No one had told him a damn thing. Not until Robert had come to him.

Disgusted, Colt took a bite of his chicken enchilada. Immediately sorry he had, Colt frowned, dropped his fork onto the bright orange food tray and reluctantly swallowed. "How can you eat this stuff?"

Robert shrugged and took another healthy bite. "It's here. I'm hungry. Case closed."

Okay, he could see that. One glance around the crowded cafeteria assured him that the hospital had a captive audience here. Most of the customers were nurses and doctors, with a handful of civilians thrown in just for good measure.

"So," Robert said as he dipped a spoon into a bowl of vegetable soup, "I've only got a half hour for lunch. What did you want to talk about?"

"Right." Colt nodded, pushed his food tray to one side and folded his arms on the table in front of him. "I understand family loyalty," he began. "So I get why you kept quiet for so long. And I know what it cost you to go against Penny's wishes to tell me the truth."

Robert sat back and pushed one hand through his hair. "It wasn't easy. Penny and I've been through a lot together. She's always been there for me and I owe her everything. But I was tired of watching her live hand to mouth."

There was something more that Robert wasn't saying. It was there in the man's eyes. He owed his sister everything? Why? What had he and Penny been through together?

"I'm not saying anything else that would betray her confidence," Robert told him. "If you want more answers, you'll have to ask her yourself. Telling you about the twins was different. You're their father. You had a right to know."

"Yeah, I did." Colt nodded tightly. He didn't like knowing that Penny had felt she couldn't come to him. Didn't like thinking about her having such a hard time. Worrying. Alone with the responsibility of raising two children.

Scrubbing one hand across the back of his neck, he pushed those thoughts aside. "Look, I came here to tell you that I'll continue to be a part of the twins' lives."

Surprise flickered across Robert's features. "Is that right? So, you're staying?"

"No," he said, the word blurting from him instinctively.

Hell, he hadn't even had to think about it. He didn't stay. Colt didn't do permanent. He always had one foot out the door because it was safer that way. Not just for him but for whoever was in his life.

"I won't be staying, but I'll be around and I'll keep in touch," Colt said flatly. "And I will see to it that your sister doesn't have to worry about money anymore."

"Uh-huh. Good to know." Robert reached for his coffee and took a long sip. "So what're you going to do about the fact that she's still in love with you?"

Colt just glared at the other man. He wasn't even going to address that statement. Mainly because he didn't know *how* to address it. He'd been avoiding even thinking about it because there was no easy answer. He knew damn well that Penny loved him. It was in her eyes every time she looked at him. And it was just another reason for him to get the hell out of her life before it was too late.

He didn't want Penny to count on him. He didn't want his kids depending on him. He'd already failed people who mattered and the aftereffects of that had nearly killed him. Ten years later, he was *still* paying for what he'd done. His dreams were still haunted by the memories that wouldn't fade. By the screams. By the thunderous roar of an avalanche and the aching wail of ambulances that were just too late.

He wouldn't chance all of that happening again. But he also wasn't going to discuss any of this with Penny's brother.

"That's none of your business," he said.

"Probably," Robert agreed. "But she's my sister."

"I get that. Family loyalty is important." Colt knew that better than most. And no matter what happened or didn't happen between him and Penny, she and the twins would always be his family. He would see that they were well taken care of. Have everything they needed. In fact, he would do anything for them.

Except stay.

Colt's house was amazing.

It sat on the tip of the bluff in Dana Point, and boasted views of the Pacific from every room in the house. Three stories of living space sprawled across the cliff side, with decks and patios jutting out at every angle. There was a grassy, tree-laden space on either side of the house, with plexiglass fences to keep people safe while still allowing for the view.

It was lush and elegant yet somehow managed to feel cozy. There were ten bedrooms, seven bathrooms and a kitchen that would bring professional chefs to tears. Everything about the place, from the architecture to its perch overlooking the ocean, was breathtaking. Yet it felt...lonely. As if it were a model home waiting to be chosen by a family. Waiting to be *lived* in.

"So," Colt asked when he joined her on the stone terrace. "What do you think?"

"It's beautiful," she said automatically, then shifted her gaze to the wide sweep of ocean stretching out in front of her. Sailboats skimmed the surface of the water, breakers churned into the shore below the house, and a handful of surfers bobbed up and down with the rhythm of the waves. "How long have you lived here?"

He leaned one hip casually against the stone railing and flicked a glance at the sea. "A few years. It's a good base for me. I like being near the ocean."

"A base," she repeated. "So, you're not here often."

"Nope." He straightened up and shoved both hands into the pockets of his jeans.

"Your housekeeper must love working for you," she murmured. "Nothing much to do really until you show up occasionally."

He grinned and she had to force her heart back down from her throat to her chest where it belonged.

"I know she's excited to have you and the twins here to take care of. It's true I'm not here much, but you know me, Penny. I keep moving."

Yes, she did know that, and it tore at her heart to admit it to herself. He was standing right beside her, tall and gorgeous, his black hair ruffled by the sea breeze, his ice-blue eyes narrowed against the sunlight, and he might as well have been in Sicily jumping off that dumb volcano. He was so far from her she felt that she would never be able to reach him.

Then she noticed that his jaw was so tight it was a wonder he didn't grind his teeth into powder. That muscle flexing in his jaw was the only outward sign that he wasn't as cool and detached as he would like her to believe.

He was on edge, too. And for some reason, that made her feel better. Good to know she wasn't in an emotional turmoil on her own.

"You get the twins settled?"

"Yes," she said with a warm smile. Remembering the nursery where she'd tucked the babies in sent shafts of tenderness for Colt dazzling through her. "I can't believe you managed to have an entire room done up for them in a few hours."

"Money can accomplish a lot of things very quickly."

Her smile deepened. He might pretend to be unmoved, even isolated, but what he'd done for his children disproved that lie. The twins' nursery here was almost an exact duplicate of their room at the cottage. Bigger, of course, with a staggering view of the ocean. But the cribs were identical, the night-light was the same, their toys and dressers, right down to stacks of new clothes and towers of diapers. All sitting there waiting for the twins to make use of them.

"Yes, your money paid for it, Colt," she said. "But it wasn't your bank account that chose the twin teddy bears or saw to it that a guardrail was installed across the window."

He frowned a little.

"That was you, Colt. You were thinking about the twins. About their safety. Their happiness."

"And that surprises you?" he asked.

"No," she said, moving closer to him, tipping her head to one side to study him. "But I think it surprised *you*.

You love them. You love your children and want the best for them."

His frown deepened a bit and he looked…uneasy.

"Don't make more of this than there is, Penny," he warned. "Of course I care about the twins. But this situation with us is temporary and you know it. Soon I'll be leaving again and—"

She didn't want to think about that. Not now. Not until she had to. Penny had been so busy trying to maintain her anger at him that letting it go now was enough to unleash the barely restrained passion she felt for this man. She knew he'd be leaving. She knew that what they had together wasn't enough to hold him. But though they didn't have a future, they did have a present. If she was bold enough to demand it.

Memories of their night together rushed into her mind and sent dizzying spirals of want and need spinning through her body. She wanted Colt King any way she could have him. And if that meant that she would later pay with pain, then she was prepared to meet the cost. What she wasn't prepared to do was waste any more time with him.

"I know."

She stopped him by laying her fingers across his mouth. She was going to lose him and she knew it. She couldn't fight his nature. She couldn't offer him the risk and the danger he seemed to crave. So instead she would accept him as he was and leave the worrying about how she would live without him for later.

"Penny…"

"The twins are napping," she said, moving in even closer, until her breasts were pressed to his chest. Until she had to tip her head back to meet the ice-blue eyes that were now burning with the kind of passion she'd only known with Colton King. "Your housekeeper is out at the store stocking your kitchen. We have the house to ourselves, Colt. Let's not waste it."

He grabbed her and pulled her tightly to him. "Do you know what you're saying?"

Watery winter sunlight spilled down around them. The sea breeze ruffled their hair and sent a chill she hardly felt down Penny's spine.

"I do. I want you, Colt. There's no point in denying it," she said, laying both hands flat against his chest. She felt the thundering gallop of his heart beneath her palm. "You want me, too. I know you do."

He didn't deny it. How could he? If anything, he held her tighter, closer, and she could feel the proof of his desire pressing into her.

"Let's enjoy what we have while we have it," she said.

"I can't stay." Colt's eyes searched hers.

"And I can't go." Penny met his gaze. "But we're both here, *now*."

For the last few days, it had taken every ounce of Colt's self-control to keep from taking Penny back to bed. He wanted her with every breath. His entire body ached with need. He walked around in a constant state of pain and discomfort. But having sex with her again would only magnify the mistake he'd already made.

Hell, he hadn't come back into her life to claim her—she deserved a hell of a lot better than *him*. He couldn't give her what she wanted. What she needed. Stability. A husband to count on. A happy family living in her dollhouse cottage surrounded by a white picket fence. It wasn't in him and he knew she'd never be happy with anything less. And why the hell should she have to settle for a sometimes man when she was worth so much more? She needed to find a man who would be beside her. Someone she could depend on.

Though the thought of another man touching her, claiming her as his own, raising his kids, sent jagged bolts of pure fury through Colt. But he didn't know what the hell else he could do. If he stayed, he'd fail them. He knew it. Felt it. And that was one risk he was unwilling to take.

"Colt," she said, fisting her hands in his T-shirt, tugging at him until he came out of his thoughts to stare into her eyes. "We have *now*," she repeated. "Let's make that enough."

He smiled and shook his head. "You're not an 'enough' kind of woman," he told her. "Penny, you're the all-or-nothing type."

"Maybe I was. But people change," she insisted.

"No, they don't." He lifted both hands to cup her face, loving the feel of her skin beneath his palms. Wishing things were different. "Situations change and people try to adapt. But at the heart of it, we are who we are. Always."

"And who are you?"

"A bad risk," he told her, his insides quaking, his voice hard.

"I'll take my chances," she said and went up on her toes to kiss him.

For a full second, maybe two, Colt didn't respond. His brain was warning him to step back for her sake if not his own. To do the right thing. To make her see that nothing good could come of this.

But her mouth was insistent. Her tongue touched his

lips and his body took over, shutting his brain down. Conscience took a backseat to need and he growled low in his throat as he returned her kiss, deepening it. His tongue tangled with hers. He tasted her breath, the sweetness of her, and swore when she wrapped her arms around his neck that he felt her soul sliding into his.

How the hell could he turn down what she suggested? She was willing to risk pain; how could he do any less? He was going to have her. Going to indulge in what she offered and then he would walk away as he knew he should. It was the only way to keep her safe. To keep their children safe.

She sighed and melted into him, breasts against his chest, mouth hungrily meeting his.

The sun continued to shine down on them with warmth, not heat, and together they built a fire between them that put that pale winter sun to shame. The sound of the waves crashing into shore hammered into the silence, sounding like a ragged heartbeat. Seagulls screeched, a soft sea breeze blew and as they remained locked together on the terrace, the world slipped past in a haze of passion.

His hands roamed up and down her body, loving the feel of her curves as he continued to plunder her mouth, taking her breath, her sighs, into himself and holding them there. She moved against him and his erection throbbed painfully against the confines of his jeans. He had to have her. There was no time for niceties. No time for subtle seduction. This was lust, pure and simple and demanding.

Breaking the kiss, he bent, swept her up into his arms and headed for the house.

"You can't carry me," she complained.

"Looks like I can," he said and never broke stride.

"God, this is romantic."

He laughed, glanced into her shining eyes and said, "Glad you think so. I think it's expedient."

"That, too." She lifted one hand to cup his face, then let it drop so she could slide one hand across his muscular chest.

Even through the fabric of his T-shirt, Colt felt the heat of her touch right down to his bones. His mind was racing, his body was on hyperdrive and all he could think was *bed*. Had to get to the closest bed.

He headed for the master bedroom and didn't stop until he'd dropped her onto the mattress. Here, the walls were glass, affording a wide, uninterrupted view of the sea. At night, he could lower electric shades that would give him privacy, but here on the bluff, they weren't really necessary. No one could see into his room unless they were in a helicopter with a pair of binoculars.

And he was suddenly grateful for that privacy. He didn't want her in darkness. He wanted her in the sunlight. He wanted to feast on the sight of Penny, to burn her image into his brain so that when he was out of her life completely, he would be able to remember this day. This moment.

Nine

She stared up at him and Colt felt as if he could drown in the green of her eyes. Her dark red hair spilled across the white pillowcase and looked like spun silk. When she sat up, he pulled her to him for another hungry kiss. When he broke it, gulping for air like a dying man, he muttered, "Clothes. Off. Now."

"Yes." Quickly, she stripped out of her clothes and lay back across the bed, arms high over her head, back arched as if offering herself to him.

His mouth went dry. He undressed faster than he ever had before. In seconds, they were tangled together on the cool, crisp sheets. Rolling together across the wide mattress, their legs entwined, flesh met flesh. Hands explored. Mouths fused. Heartbeats hammered in tandem.

Sunlight flashed in and out from behind thick gray clouds scuttling across the sky. The French doors to the patio stood open and a cool, soft wind blew into the room, caressing heated skin.

Colt pinned her to the mattress, gave her a slow, seductive smile and dipped his head to take first one, then the other nipple into his mouth. Her scent filled his mind. The soft sighs she made fed the desire licking at his insides and pushed him on, wanting more, needing more. Lips, tongue and teeth teased her, toyed with her until she was writhing beneath him, gasping his name.

Hunger pitched higher in them both and he swept one hand down the length of her body to dip his fingers into her slick, wet heat. She lifted her hips and rocked into his touch, setting a rhythm that threw Colt's control down a slippery slope. He wanted. Needed. He felt her desire as his own and let the heat consume them both. He gave himself up to the fire within, jumping eagerly into the flames.

He looked her over, head to toe, and seared the image onto his brain. Sunlight dancing on pale skin. A few golden freckles lying dark against that paleness and the thatch of dark red hair at the juncture of her thighs. Perfection. She was all. She was everything. His heart stuttered in his chest as new and unexpected realizations rose up in his mind. Deliberately, he shut his brain off, letting his body take over. He didn't want to think now. Didn't want to acknowledge anything beyond this moment.

The only thing that mattered now was feeding the beast crouched inside both their bodies. He pulled his hand from her heat and she whimpered at the loss.

"Don't stop," she said on a heaving sigh. "Don't you dare stop."

"Not stopping, trust me," he managed to grind out. He couldn't have stopped touching her if it had meant his life. The feel of her beneath his hands, the flick of her tongue over her bottom lip and the glazed passion in her eyes all came together to twist him into knots so tight they might never come undone.

He flipped her over onto her stomach and ran his hands up and down her spine, cupping the curve of her incredible behind. She parted her legs, tossed her hair out of her way to look over her shoulder at him and whispered, "Oh, yes."

As if he'd needed any encouragement.

She licked her lips again as if she knew what that action did to him and enjoyed the power of it. Then she went up on her knees, silently inviting him to take what they both wanted so badly.

Her behind was full and curvy and he smoothed both hands over her soft flesh, kneading, exploring. He slid one hand down to cup her heat and she groaned, pushing into him, wiggling hips that drove him crazy.

"Don't make me wait, Colt. Don't make *us* wait. Take me where only you can," she whispered, desire-filled, forest-green eyes fixed on him.

"Oh, yeah." His voice was scratchy, words pushing through the knot lodged in his throat. He knelt behind her, pulled her in close and entered her in one long, smooth stroke.

She gasped in pleasure and he barely heard the soft sound over his own groan of satisfaction. She was tight and hot and he had to get a grip on the lust nearly choking him or he would explode in an instant.

Penny moved into him, wriggling those hips again, pushing back against him, taking him deeper, higher, and he felt every one of her movements like a caress. He moved into her, retreating and advancing, following the frantic rhythm set by his own heartbeat. He heard her gasps, her whispered moans. He felt her passion climb with his. He held her hips in a firm grip and set a pace that she hurried to follow.

Again and again, they climbed together, reaching for the peak that awaited them. And when he felt the first tremor begin inside her, he reached around to where their bodies were joined and thumbed the sensitive spot that held so many fragmented sensations.

She turned her face into the mattress and cried out, her shriek of pleasure muted but no less rousing. And an instant later, Colt followed her, jumping into the void with her, holding her close as shards of light and shadow erupted all around them.

A few minutes later, with Penny tucked close to his side and sunlight dancing in the room, Colt's old fears rose up to gnaw on him again.

He loved her. Loved her as he'd never believed it possible to love.

He couldn't tell her. She would expect…what she had every right to expect from a man who loved her. But he couldn't give her what she wanted. Needed. He couldn't take that chance.

Panic reared its ugly head, but he fought it down. His gaze locked on the small scar from the operation she'd so recently had. She was almost healed completely. And when that happened, he would leave her. As he'd known all along that he would.

Love. He didn't even want to think the word. It left him vulnerable. Worse, having him love her made Penny vulnerable and that he couldn't stand. Instead of being the blessing that most people might consider it, Colt knew that love wasn't for him. That ephemeral feeling only fed the deep-seated guilt and shame that were never far from his thoughts.

Penny sighed, nestled her head on his chest and draped one long, shapely leg across him. And even as he drew her closer, Colt began to plan his escape.

Over the next several days, Penny and Colt fell into a routine. They tag-teamed the twins and she had to admit, at least to herself, that life with two babies was infinitely easier when you had someone who could share the work *and* the fun.

Of course, whenever that thought appeared in her mind, Penny did her best to ignore it. Love filled her, but had nowhere to go. She wanted to trust him, but she knew that Colt wouldn't stay. He'd made that clear from the beginning. So she locked her love up deep inside her where he couldn't see it. Where she wouldn't be reminded of it daily.

She tried instead to simply enjoy this time with him while she had it. And when he was gone, she'd learn to go on without him. Again.

They left Colt's spectacular house on the cliff and moved the twins back home. Penny loved the cottage, always would, but now she saw the limitations of it. Oh, it was filled with good memories and it was perfect for her and the twins—at the moment. One day, she'd have to leave because the house would be too small. It wouldn't fit her growing family. So the cottage was pretty much like her and Colt. Perfect in the present but no promise of a future.

Penny thought about Colt's place and couldn't help wondering how things might have been. At the cliff house, there had been laughter and passion and so much sky and sea and lawn—open and beautiful. But it wasn't the house she missed so much as the closeness she and Colt had found there, and she knew it. It didn't matter that they spent their nights together now, making love and exploring their passions.

Because every day, she felt him slipping further and further away from her. Soon, even though he might be standing in her tiny kitchen, he would be too far away to touch.

Knowing that broke her heart, but there was nothing she could do about it.

When the twins had been fed their lunch and put down for a much-needed afternoon nap, Penny found Colt in the living room, staring down at the small fire he'd lit only an hour before. Flames crackled over wood and sparks shot up the chimney like tiny fireworks.

Outside, the day was cold and dark, threatening rain that Southern California desperately needed. Inside, despite the fire burning merrily, the cold was creeping in to encircle them both.

"The twins asleep?" he asked without tearing his gaze from the dancing flames.

"Yes. When they take a ride in the car they're always ready to conk out when they get home." It hadn't been much of a trip, she thought. Just to the grocery store. But it was good to be getting back into her routine. Good to remind herself that even when Colt was gone, she would still have her life. Her children's lives. Everything wouldn't end when he left.

It would just be…emptier.

"You should have told me you needed to get groceries," he said, gaze still locked on the fire.

"Why would I do that?" she asked. "It was just groceries. I do it all the time."

Penny sat down on the worn sofa and stared at him. Even from the back, she could tell that he was upset. Every line of his body radiated tension. Frowning, she asked, "What's wrong?"

Finally, he turned his head and speared her with a hard look out of narrowed blue eyes. "What's *wrong?* I go to the office for two hours, then get back here just in time to find you carrying heavy grocery bags, not to mention the twins, and you want to know what's wrong?"

Confused, she said, "Who do you think does it when you're not here, Colt? Me. I also do laundry and mow lawns. What's the big deal?"

"The big deal is," he said through gritted teeth, as if he were struggling to hold on to his temper, "you've had surgery. You shouldn't be lifting anything heavy until the doctor gives you the go-ahead."

Defending herself and her own choices, she said, "I see him in a few days and by the way, I feel fine. Hardly even sore anymore."

"That's not the point."

"Well, what *is* the point then?"

He blew out a breath, pushed one hand through his hair and turned to face her. His blue eyes looked hard and remote and something inside Penny tightened. She recognized that look in his eyes. She'd seen it once before. The morning after their marriage when he'd announced that it was over and walked away from her.

So it had come, she thought sadly. He was leaving again. And she wasn't ready to lose him. She wouldn't ever be ready.

"I don't like you having to do everything yourself,"

Colt was saying. "I'm here now, you know? You could have waited for me to get back."

"Waited for you, Colt?" she whispered, her voice nearly lost in the hiss and crackle of the fire. "How long? How long should I wait?"

"What're you talking about?" he asked. "You knew I was going into the office to take care of a few things and then I'd be back."

Her heart ached and a ball of ice dropped into the pit of her stomach. "I never know if you're coming back, Colt," she admitted quietly. "Every time you go out, I wonder if this is the time that you'll just keep going."

"What? Why?"

She hunched her shoulders and blew out a breath. "Because we both know you're going to leave. The only thing I don't know is *when*."

Colt's lips thinned into a straight, grim line. "This isn't about me, Penny. It's about you. You do too much."

"How much is too much?" she argued, feeling the need to defend the way she lived her life. "I have two babies to take care of."

"Yeah," he muttered thickly, "I know, but you should have help."

She'd had help. From him. Now he was taking that help away and wanted to replace himself with…what? "Help?"

"I can hire a nanny. Or a housekeeper," he offered quickly. "Someone to take some of the load off of your shoulders."

"You want to *hire* someone?" Penny sat up straighter and met his gaze. She could see the distance in his blue eyes. She actually *felt* him putting up a wall between them, shutting her out.

"Yeah. What's wrong with that?"

"Throwing money at a problem isn't the only answer," she said.

"Give me another one," he countered.

"Stay."

Oh, God, the moment that word left her mouth she wanted to pull it back in. Wanted to pretend she'd never said it, especially when she saw shutters drop over Colt's eyes.

"We've been over this. I can't stay."

"You say that but you don't tell me *why*." She jumped up from the sofa and faced him.

"And you won't tell me why you won't accept the help I can offer you."

"Because I don't want your money, Colt." All she wanted was his love, and she wasn't going to get that. "Or your guilt."

He shook his head, threw his hands high and let them slap down against his thighs. "What's guilt got to do with anything?"

"Do you think I can't see it?" Penny took a step closer to him. "You're getting ready to leave so you want to make sure you've covered all of your bases. It's like you have a mental list. Help for Penny, check. Nanny for the twins, check. Money in her bank account, check. And once you've completed that list, you can leave with a clear conscience. Well, forget it. If I need help I'll ask for it."

"No, you won't." He laughed shortly and gave her a look that told her he was far from amused. "You think you've got me all figured out, huh? Well, I know you just as well, Penny. You're too stubborn for your own good. You hate accepting help. Don't want to lean on anyone."

That verbal slap struck a nerve and Penny felt the

sting of tears at the backs of her eyes. She blinked hard and fast, because she wasn't about to cry. He was pulling away from her with every passing moment and had the nerve to accuse her of not wanting to depend on him?

"Why should I lean on anyone, Colt?" she asked, her voice hardly more than a whisper of old pain. "I've been taking care of myself for most of my life. I grew up taking care of myself and Robert. No one was there to help."

He frowned. "Your parents?"

Shadows in the room gathered closer. The flickering light of the fire danced on the walls and reflected in the window panes. The world slipped away until it was only Penny, Colt and the past crowded into the tiny living room.

"When my mom died ten years ago, my father just shut down. He went to work, came home, but he was like a ghost in the house." It sounded so cut-and-dried when she said it, but the memories of her childhood were still with her. Still painful. When her mother died, Penny was eighteen. She felt lost and turned to her father, but he couldn't or wouldn't give her the emotional support she needed so badly. She'd had to learn how to stand up. How to be a rock for Robert and how to take care of herself.

"I couldn't lean on my father," she said hotly. "I couldn't trust him. Sometimes he came home, sometimes he didn't. So I took care of myself and Robert. And the day I turned eighteen my dad took off for good and we haven't seen him since." She poked her index finger at the center of his chest. "So don't tell me that I'm too stubborn to ask for help. It's not stubbornness, it's survival. I don't trust easily, Colt, and I learned early that it's easier in the long run to not depend on anyone but yourself."

Her breath was coming in short, hard pants and she

kept her gaze fixed on his, so she saw the shadow of sympathy in his eyes. Penny's spine went stiff and straight and she lifted her chin defiantly. "I don't need you to feel sorry for me, either."

"I wasn't."

She folded her arms over her chest, cocked her head at a mocking tilt and studied him.

"Okay," he admitted, "maybe I was. Not for who you are now, but for the girl you were, with so much responsibility dumped on you."

"I survived."

"Yeah, but it affected you." He shook his head. "You tell me I take too many risks, but you don't take any, do you? If you don't trust people they can't let you down. Is that it?"

She shifted position uncomfortably. Maybe that was a little too close to home. "I trusted you once."

He ground his teeth together until she saw the muscle in his jaw flexing furiously.

Shaking her head, Penny said, "Our situations are different, Colt. You risk your life constantly. I don't want to risk trusting the wrong person. Big difference."

"This isn't even about trust," he countered, blowing out a breath. "Or what's between us. This is about you accepting help. You've already proven you *can* do everything on your own, Penny. That doesn't mean you *have* to."

She laughed a little but there was no humor in the sound. "You don't get it. Who is there to lean on, Colt? Robert? He and Maria are building their own lives. They don't need me hanging around being needy. You?" She sighed. "Why would I lean on you when you've made no secret of the fact that you're leaving just as fast you can?"

"You could while I'm here," he started to argue.

"Why would I get used to help from you, Colt?" She reached up and shoved both hands through her hair as frustration grabbed hold of her and refused to let go. "You arrived here with your bags packed emotionally. You've had one foot out the door for this entire time. So tell me. Should I count on you, Colt? Should I depend on you?"

"No." He cut her off abruptly and Penny was so surprised her mouth snapped shut. Briefly.

"Well, at least that was honest," she choked out as she wrapped her arms around her middle and held on.

Colt looked at her and not for the first time thought she was one of the strongest people he'd ever known. Now that he knew more of her background, he was even more impressed. No wonder Robert had said he owed Penny everything. She'd raised him. She'd kept him safe. And she'd done it on her own with no help from anyone.

Hell, he hadn't wanted her to depend on him and it should make him feel good that she had no intention of counting on Colt for anything. Instead, he felt worse than ever. He wished to hell he could just grab her, pull her close and never let her go. But that wasn't gonna happen. Couldn't happen.

Pulling back from her and the kids was the right thing to do and he knew it.

But clearly Penny believed he simply didn't want to stay. That bothered him more than he wanted to admit. So if he told her the truth, then not only would she understand, she'd agree that his leaving was the best thing for all of them.

"You think I don't want to be here."

"I think you can't wait to leave. Just like before," she said sadly.

"You're wrong."

"Then prove it," she countered. "Stay."

"No," he said tiredly, feeling old guilt and the shadows of pain he'd never allowed to die swamp him.

"This is ridiculous. You're not *telling* me anything. Just like before, you're going to walk away. And I'm supposed to believe that what? You're leaving for *my* sake? Because if that's it," Penny snapped, "then don't do me any favors."

"I'm trying to keep you and the twins alive and safe." He grabbed her upper arms and barely held back from giving her a hard shake. "You think it's easy for me to walk away? It's not. But if I stay, then somewhere down the line, everything's going to go to hell."

"What's that supposed to mean?" Her eyes were locked on his, confusion and fury glittering in those green depths. She was amazing and he wanted her more than his next breath.

Deliberately, he let her go and took a step back from her. Swiping one hand across his face, he muttered, "It was ten years ago."

"What?"

He looked away from her because how the hell could he look into her eyes while he said, "I was in Switzerland with my folks. Supposed to be a big ski trip." His voice sounded as haunted as his dreams. Colt closed his eyes briefly, but the images from the past were so clear, so sharp, they nearly killed him. So he opened his eyes again and stared down into the fire.

"We were supposed to take a helicopter to the top of a peak and then ski down. But the night before the run,

I met some blonde in a bar—" he stopped and realized "—I can't even remember her name. Point is, I blew off the ski trip in favor of spending time with the blonde. My parents died in an avalanche."

He turned to face her and realized that now it was his turn to read the sympathy in her eyes and he found he liked it no better than she had. Shoving his hands into his jeans pockets, he shook his head wearily. "I let them down. They were depending on me to show them the safe route down the mountain and I wasn't there."

"Colt, I'm so sorry but—"

He shook his head. "Don't tell me it wasn't my fault. I know it was. If I'd been there, they wouldn't have died because I could have steered them to a safer run."

"Or," Penny argued, "you would have died with them."

"Maybe." He'd thought of that, too, and sometimes wondered if he wouldn't have been better off. He pulled his hands free of his pockets and scrubbed both hands over his face. She was still watching him and the urge to hold her was so strong it rocked him. But if he touched her, then he'd lose himself in the flash of heat and passion that threatened to consume everything in its path. And it wouldn't change a damn thing.

"It was an accident, Colt," she said firmly. "Not a reason for you to run from me or your kids."

"Weren't you listening?" He shook his head. "I'm not running. It's not me I'm worried about. It's whoever depends on me. I let my folks down and they died. I won't do that to my kids. Or you. I won't live with even more of the kind of guilt that chews on a man when he fails."

Penny lifted both hands and shoved them through her hair in an impatient gesture. "So, basically," she said tightly, "instead of failing, you just don't try at all."

"You don't understand what it's like."

"Yeah, I do," she said, voice breaking until she swallowed hard and took a breath. "You know, over this last week or so, I've watched you with the twins. Seen how good you are with them. How much they love you."

His heart clenched hard in his chest.

"And I tried to figure out why, when you have so much in your life, you insist on flying off around the globe chasing death in those ridiculous extreme sports." She scrubbed her hands along her upper arms as if trying to create warmth that just wouldn't come. "Now I know. Are you trying to make it up to your parents by dying? Is that it? Do you think you've been on borrowed time or something? That you should have been the one to die on that mountain?"

"I didn't say that," he argued.

"You might as well have." Penny glared at him and Colt felt his hackles rise. Damn it, he'd expected her to get it. To finally understand why nothing could work between them. Instead, she was staring at him like he was crazy.

"Let me get this straight," she finally said, tipping her head back to meet his eyes. "You want me to lean on you and at the same time you tell me you don't want anyone to depend on you. That about cover it?"

He scrubbed one hand across his jaw, then the back of his neck. It sounded…stupid when she said it like that. Irritated and getting angrier and more defensive by the moment, Colt said, "You're deliberately twisting my words around."

"No, I'm not," she countered and stepped closer, tapping his chest with her forefinger. "I'm pointing out that what you're telling me doesn't make any sense."

"It does to me," he managed to grind out. "I'm the reason my parents died. If I'd been there—"

She cut him off. "You'll never know what might have happened if you had been there, Colt. But the point is, you didn't cause the avalanche. It was an accident. A tragic, horrible accident. But you didn't do it. You weren't even there."

"That's the point," he snapped. "I promised them I would be and I wasn't."

"And I bet your mother's last thoughts were, 'Thank God Colt isn't here.'"

He jerked his head back as if she'd slapped him.

"It's what I would have thought," she continued, her voice softer now. "What I would have been grateful for. That my child was safe. How can you believe your parents would have thought differently?"

He spun away from her, his mind racing, heart pounding. He'd lived with the guilt for so long that it was a part of him. A dark shadow that crouched inside his heart always ready to take a stab at him.

"It must have been hideous, Colt," she said, threading her arms around his waist, pressing herself against his back. "But it doesn't change the fact that it wasn't your fault."

Con had said the same thing for years. So had his other brothers. His cousins. But, "No matter what you say, it doesn't change the fact that I wasn't there when they needed me."

He turned in her arms, looked down into her eyes and vowed, "I won't risk it again. Won't let you or the twins depend on me because it'd kill me if something happened to any of you."

"And if something happens anyway? Then what?"

Tears glistened in her eyes and the light from the fire made the dampness there gleam with a red-hot glow.

Slowly, she stepped back from him and stuffed her hands into the pockets of her worn, faded jeans, as if trying to keep from reaching out to him again. "Don't you see? Nobody gets a guarantee in life, Colt. All we have is every day and the people we choose to spend our lives with—for however long that is. You're not to blame for what happened to your parents, Colt. But maybe it's easier for you to tell yourself you are."

"Easy?" Voice tight and hard, he said, "You think anything about this is easy?"

"It's always easier to walk away than to stay and make it work."

"I told you—"

"I know what you told me," she said, mouth twisting as she fought trembling lips. "But you were wrong. You didn't escape that avalanche, Colt. Something in you died that day up on the mountain."

Outrage swelled up inside him. Hell, he'd expected her to get it. To understand and see that he was doing this for her and the twins. To protect them the one sure way he knew how. But she was standing there glaring at him through eyes that had gone as cold and dark as a forest at midnight. "Penny, damn it, don't you see—"

"Are you supposed to pay penance for the rest of your life, Colt? For something that wasn't your fault?" Penny shook her head, met his gaze and held it. "Is that the price you have to pay to satisfy the ghosts in your heart? You're not allowed to be happy? Not allowed to be loved?"

"This isn't penance," he argued. "This is me trying to protect you and the twins. Why don't you see that?"

"What I see is that it's time for you to go, Colt. Just

leave." She pulled her hands free of her pockets and used them both to push back her thick mane of hair. "You would have left soon anyway, so go tonight. I don't want my children to love a father who's so busy trying to kill himself that he's forgotten how to *live*."

Ten

Colt didn't stick around. What would have been the point? He threw his stuff together and left while the twins were still sleeping because God help him, he didn't think he could walk out the door with his kids watching him go. His kids.

Those two words bounced around in his skull like maniacal rubber balls. He never had bothered to get a paternity test. He hadn't needed to. He'd known in his gut the moment he'd seen them that those babies were *his*. Just as he knew now that he had to leave.

He just hadn't expected Penny to be the one to tell him to go. Damn it, *he* was the one who left. Always. No woman before her had ever asked him to leave. Though he supposed she had reason enough.

"The problem is she doesn't get it," he muttered, and drove down the Pacific Coast Highway not even noticing the ocean on his right. "How could she? She's never failed anyone before."

He had, though. His mind spun darkly through all the memories he'd just dug up and stomped through.

"Never should have tried to explain," he told himself, pushing dark thoughts aside to concentrate on the road and the wild race of his heartbeat. "Should have just gone. Should never have stayed that long in the first damn place."

But how could he not? He had *kids*. Two tiny human beings who were alive because of him and they deserved…what?

"Better than a part-time father, that's what," he muttered as he turned his car onto the private road that led to the house on the cliff.

He slapped one hand against the steering wheel, then waved at the security guard at the gate. He drove past in a hurry and followed the narrow, winding road to his driveway. When he got there, he stopped, parked and reluctantly turned off the engine.

What he wanted to do was to keep driving. To push his car and himself to their limits. To feel that rush of speed that came when you discarded the idea of being careful. When you raced out to stay just ahead of—

He stopped that thought cold as Penny's voice echoed in his mind. *Chasing death. Forgotten how to live.*

She was wrong, though, he argued silently. He wasn't chasing death, for God's sake. He was relishing every moment of his life. He wasn't wasting time. He wasn't going to be an old man and regret not taking chances. Not living life to the fullest. That's what this was about. *Life,* not *death*.

But Penny's voice wouldn't leave his mind. Her accusatory stare seemed to drill right into his soul. And the look on her face when she told him to leave the cottage would stay with him forever.

From the moment he'd met Penny, he had known that this woman wasn't the kind you could forget. And he hadn't. Now the memories of her were thicker, richer, more deeply embedded in his soul. Somehow, she'd become a part of him and leaving her had felt as though he was carving out his own heart with a butter knife.

Hands fisted on the steering wheel, he sat in the shade of the spectacular house that hadn't become a home until Penny and the twins had arrived. He looked up at the building and felt an emptiness he'd never known before. He was being chased not only by his own past but by the futures that he wouldn't be a part of.

He already missed Penny. The scent of her. The sound of her laugh. The taste of her. Colt had never thought about falling in love. Never even considered it. But now he realized that when he'd first met her in Vegas, he'd instinctively known that she would be the one woman he would never get over.

Now he'd made that situation worse.

Then there were the twins. He didn't want to think about all he would miss with his kids, but how could he help it? First words. First steps. First day of school. First heartbreak. He'd miss them all.

His heart twisted in his chest, but he couldn't back down now. He was doing the right thing and he'd keep on doing it. Even if he suffered every day of his life because he'd walked away from the three people in the world who meant the most to him.

Grabbing his duffel bag, Colt climbed out of the car, slung the bag over one shoulder and headed inside. What he needed to do was to get back to the real world. The exciting race to find bigger and better adrenaline rushes.

The house was too quiet. Deliberately, he didn't notice a thing about the place where Penny and the twins had been so recently. They'd left themselves stamped all over the house, but he figured the memories would fade in time. And if they didn't, he'd sell the damn house.

He made a few phone calls—his brother, the airport and his lawyer—threw some clothes in another bag, then grabbed up his ski equipment and headed for John Wayne Airport. A KingJet would be waiting for him and in several hours, he'd be where he should have gone nearly two weeks ago. Sicily. Mount Etna.

He'd reclaim normalcy for himself and chalk up the last couple of weeks as a glitch on his radar. A bump in the road.

Which would be much easier to do if the memory of Penny's eyes would just leave him the hell alone.

Both of the twins were whiny and Penny knew just how they felt. They missed Colt and so did she. In a couple of short weeks, he'd become a part of their lives in the cottage, and now that he was gone, there was an aching hole in the tapestry of their family.

She still couldn't believe that she'd actually *told* him to leave the night before. After wishing so hard that he would stay, it was completely ironic that she would be the one to tell him to go.

She'd been awake all night, going over their conversation, word for word. She remembered the shadowed look in his eyes when he'd told her about the day his parents died. She'd seen the pain and the guilt glittering in his gaze despite his effort to shield his emotions from her.

Penny knew he was hurt and had been for years. She felt bad for him, living with misplaced guilt for so long, but at the same time she wanted to shriek at him. He hadn't killed his family. Why did he have to keep suffering? When would it be enough?

She'd overcome her past and moved on. Why couldn't he? Why couldn't he value her and their children more than his own fears and guilt? And why was she still torturing herself?

Her baby girl let out a snuffle and a cry and Penny immediately turned her brain back to matters at hand.

"It's okay, Riley," she soothed as she changed her daughter's T-shirt. "I know you miss your daddy, but it'll get easier, I promise."

Lies. Why did parents always lie to their children? It wasn't going to get easier. It would never be easy living without Colt. The twins were lucky, she supposed; they were too young to carry this memory with them. She knew that Colt would come back for the kids. That he would visit them and remain a part of their lives. But it was just a shadow of what they might have had together.

"I never should have told him," Robert said from the open doorway of the kids' room. "I'm really sorry, Pen. I thought he'd do the right thing."

"Don't be sorry," she said and tugged a clean shirt over Riley's head. The baby girl laughed and clapped her chubby hands in appreciation. Penny glanced at her brother. "Colt had the right to know about the twins and now he does. Let's just leave it at that."

"Sure. It's no problem at all that he's gone, is it?"

"Nope. Life marches on, or something equally as clichéd and profound." Penny told herself she should probably worry. She was getting entirely too good at the whole lying thing. Scooping her daughter up for a hug, Penny held the baby tightly, then turned to face Robert, who was watching her with an all-too-knowing gaze.

"It never would have worked," she said, because she'd been telling herself that since the afternoon before when she'd practically tossed Colt out of her house. But she hadn't had a choice, right? He as much as told her that he wouldn't love her. Told her he couldn't be depended on. So what else could she have done?

"We're too different. He takes too many risks and I—"

"Don't take any?" Robert finished for her.

Irritated, she said, "Now you sound like Colt."

"Not surprising. It's pretty obvious, Pen." He moved farther into the room, plucked Riley out of her arms and held his niece close. "Dad did a real number on you when he left. You think I was too young to notice, but I wasn't. I watched how hard you worked to pick up the slack."

Her eyes filled with tears and she used the tips of her fingers to wipe them away. Those years had been terrifying, but satisfying, too. She'd discovered that fear didn't have to hold you back. She'd found her passion for photography. She'd seen Robert get a full scholarship to college—and then she'd met Colt and it had felt, for a while, as if she had finally found some magic for herself.

But that dream had ended and a new one, she assured herself, had begun. In the middle of all this pain and misery, she had to remember that she wasn't alone. She had her children. She had Robert and Maria. And one day, maybe that would all seem like enough.

When the ache for Colt finally faded.

"I saw how badly Dad leaving hurt you. You kind of closed yourself off, Penny. To everyone but me."

Her gaze snapped to his and she felt a flush rise up and

stain her cheeks. Maybe she had, she silently conceded. But she'd opened herself up to Colt eighteen months ago. She had taken a risk with her heart and she'd lost.

"But I saw you with Colt and you were happier than I've ever known you to be. Plus," he added, after kissing the top of Riley's head, "I know he cares about you so I hoped…"

Penny's heart twisted in her chest. She'd hoped, too. In spite of everything, she had hoped. Now she missed Colt so much. It was infinitely harder to lose him now than it had been eighteen months ago. Seeing him walk out the door, not knowing if he'd ever walk back in. Knowing that her kids would be cheated out of a day-to-day relationship with their father. That the man she loved was more interested in waiting to die than he was in living with her. It was all so hard.

"I appreciate that," she said when she was sure her voice wouldn't break. Reaching out, she smoothed Riley's wispy hair and straightened the tiny pink bow lying tilted on the side of her head. "But it's over now and I just have to learn to live with the reality."

Robert put his arm around her and she gratefully went into a warm hug meant to comfort and soothe. Riley patted her face as if the baby girl knew her mommy needed the extra attention. In the living room, she could hear Reid laughing with Maria and in spite of the giant hole in her heart, Penny smiled. And she would keep smiling, for the sake of her kids if nothing else.

"If he comes back, what will you do?"

"He won't." Even her hopes weren't strong enough to convince her of that.

"He came back once," Robert reminded her. "And it wasn't just for the kids. You didn't see his face when

I told him you were in the hospital. He cares, Penny. A lot more than he knows, I think. So yeah. He might come back again if he thought you were willing to take a chance."

How could she open herself up to trusting Colt? She had taken that leap of faith once and he'd walked away from her and their newborn marriage. If she risked it again, she wouldn't be the only one to suffer. She would be putting her children's hearts on the line, too, and she didn't know if she could do that.

"No, Robert," she said firmly, trying to convince not only her brother, but herself. The sooner she accepted the hard truth, the sooner she could start dealing with the pain that was already swamping her. She wished things were different, but wishing wasn't going to change a thing. "He's not coming back. Not this time."

But if he ever did, she would gladly take that risk again.

Colt's heart felt like a stone, cold and hard in his chest.

It was as though he'd been emptied out. He'd spilled his darkest secrets and shame and Penny had dismissed it all. For some damn reason, he'd expected her at least to understand what it cost him to go.

But she hadn't.

Her words were still ringing in Colt's ears two days later. He tried to pretend she hadn't been right but how could he? He lived his life with one foot out the door at all times. More than three weeks in one place and the walls started closing in on him. He had been in constant motion for ten years. Never staying put. Never settling down. Most important, never allowing anyone to depend on him for anything.

Now it killed him to know that Penny *refused* to depend on him.

"She's right," he mumbled, "it doesn't make any sense at all."

The jet's engine was a steady, throaty roar of background noise that seemed to rumble through his brain, which was jostling already chaotic thoughts. On the way to Sicily at last, Colt realized that normally, he'd have a map of the area spread out in front of him. He'd be laying out his plans for the trip—feeling that rush of anticipation that had been his near-constant companion for the last ten years. Today, though, there was nothing.

Just the solitude inside the jet and his own misery. He couldn't bring himself to care about Mount Etna or the challenge of skiing down the wicked slopes of a very active volcano. Instead, he could only wonder what Penny and the twins were doing. Had she gone back to the doctor? Had Reid started talking? Was Riley crawling through every mud puddle in the backyard?

Did they miss him?

Colt sprawled on one of the gray leather couches and stared out the window. Travel time was long, going from Orange County, California, to Italy. First to New York, then refuel and on to Sicily. From the airport in Catania, he'd take a helicopter to Mount Etna and do what he'd come to do: ski down the sharp face of a volcano on the verge of eruption. His gaze fixed on the clouds that lay stretched out like a path across the sky. Far below was Italy, a blur of green and brown. He hardly noticed the view, though.

Instead, he was seeing Penny's face. Hearing her voice asking him why he was chasing death. Saying that his mother had no doubt been *grateful* that he wasn't on the mountain on that fateful day. And though it had pissed him off then, he'd had time enough to think about it now and reluctantly he had to admit that Penny was right. If it had been him, caught by an avalanche, in those last few minutes, he would have been grateful that his kids would still live on. That Penny was safe.

You've forgotten how to live.

He scrubbed one hand across his face, but the action did nothing to wipe away the echoes of her voice or the image of her face. Was she right about that, too? Had he been trying to die to make it up to his parents for failing them? He squirmed uncomfortably. Sounded so damned stupid. So…pointless.

By spending so much time running from life, he'd been pretty much dead already, hadn't he?

Jumping to his feet, Colt paced up and down the length of the private jet. Having the luxury of a plane to himself was something he usually enjoyed. Today, not so much. Being alone made it impossible to avoid all of the conflicting thoughts crashing in his mind. He'd been running for so long that the thought of…standing still was almost unthinkable. But what had running gotten him?

He stopped in front of the wet bar, poured a generous splash of scotch into a crystal tumbler and drained it like medicine. Liquid fire rushed through his system, momentarily chasing away the chill icing his bones. Maybe he'd been coming at this all wrong from the beginning. Maybe he'd wasted ten years of his life chasing risk, and he'd never even noticed that he wasn't running *toward* anything. Instead he was running *away* from the greatest risk of all.

Love.

Risking death was nothing, he told himself. Risking

a life with someone was the real step that took courage. And while he held himself back, Penny took that chance. She was strong in spite of what she'd gone through when she was a kid. How could he be less?

Slamming the glass down onto the bar top, he stalked to the closest window and looked down on the world below. In his mind, the image of Mount Etna rose up, snowy peaks, smoking calderas. Then right beside that image was the memory of Penny's eyes when he was inside her. The warmth, the love, the promise of everything shining in those green depths.

Life? Or death?

No contest, he realized with a jolt. He didn't need a damn volcano to challenge him. Living with a woman as strong as Penny was going to be the *real* adventure. If, he thought, he could convince her to let him prove himself to her. To let him back into her life. Their kids' lives. But he couldn't very well do that from Sicily, could he?

He strode to the cockpit and opened the door.

The copilot turned in his seat and smiled.

Colt ignored the friendly gesture. "Where exactly are we?"

"We'll be landing at Catania, Sicily, in about an hour."

"Right." Colt nodded and for the first time in ten long years, listened to his heart. He knew what he had to do. Knew what he *wanted* to do. Decision made, he said, "When we land, refuel as quickly as you can. We're going back."

After the longest plane ride of his life, Colt stormed into King's Extreme Adventures and walked into his twin's office without bothering to knock.

"I thought you were in Sicily." Con sat back in his desk chair, a surprised expression on his face.

"Yeah, change of plans," Colt said and paced to the wide window that overlooked the ocean. "Tell me something. You've always said that mom and dad's accident wasn't my fault. Did you mean it?"

"Of course I meant it." Con's voice was sharp and sure. "What's this about?"

Down below, at street level, waves rushed toward shore, cars lined the Pacific Coast Highway and pedestrians wandered up and down crowded sidewalks.

"Penny." Colt shook his head and rubbed his eyes. His twin, his brothers and his cousins had all tried to reach him over the years. Tried to make him see that accidents happen and no matter how hideous it had all been, it wasn't Colt's fault. But he'd never been willing to listen before. Now he had to know. "She's got me thinking. Wondering. And I need to know if that's really how you and all of the others feel."

Con's voice was soft, but the power behind the words reverberated in the air. "Colt, *you* didn't cause the avalanche. Even you don't have superpowers."

Smiling briefly, Colt glanced at his twin. "If I'd been there, though, I could've made sure they took a safer run."

Con laughed shortly, then shrugged. "I don't know whose parents you're remembering, but our father never took the safe route in his life."

Colt frowned as Con stood up and came toward him. "Your being with them wouldn't have changed anything. Dad was just as damned crazy adventurous as you are— where do you think you got it?"

Colt had never really thought about it like that. But now that he was…he wondered.

"The only thing that would have been different," Con added, slapping his twin on the shoulder, "is that *you* would have died, too. And I'd have missed you, you big idiot."

A small smile curved Colt's mouth. All of the Kings did go for adventure, thrived on adrenaline, he thought, as he finally began to let go of the cloak of guilt he'd been wrapped in for years. "You're right. About Dad, I mean."

Con applauded slowly, deliberately, and gave his twin a smile. "Well, at long last. And it only took ten years to convince you. I always said I was the smart one."

"Funny." Colt drew a breath and knew that it would take time to finally and completely let go of the past. But at least now he had a shot at it. "Look, I'm going out to Penny's place. But I've got a few things to do first. One of which is to talk to you about an idea I had on the flight home."

Curious, Con grinned. "I'm listening…."

Penny missed Colt more than she would have thought it possible to miss anyone. The twins did, too, she could tell. They weren't as boisterous as usual and every once in a while, one or both of them would look around an empty room as if searching for their father. Though it broke her heart, she knew that soon, the babies would get past that sensation of something being gone from their lives. They'd go on and their memories would fade and one day, when Colt dropped back into their lives, they would look at him like a stranger.

She only wished it would be that easy for her, but she knew she would never get past this. She would long for him, dream of him for the rest of her life. In the middle of the night, she reached for him. She listened for the deep rumble of his voice as he read to the twins before bedtime. She even missed hearing him curse under his breath when he hit his head on the door frame.

That stupid man had left a giant hole in her life. And what she wouldn't give to have him back.

"You're just pitiful, that's all there is to it," she muttered, and picked up her digital camera. Turning it on, she pulled up the menu and then began flipping through the photos she'd taken during the time Colt was with them.

Colt bathing the twins, more water on him than in the tub. Colt holding a sleeping Riley, stacking blocks with Reid. Colt smiling up at Penny from the bed they'd shared too briefly. Her heart didn't just ache—it throbbed. Pain was her new best friend, and she had a feeling it wasn't going to get any easier any time soon.

Thankfully, just as she was ready to sink into the self-pity party of the year, the doorbell rang, which gave her an excuse to turn off the camera and get back to her life. With the twins asleep, she didn't want to risk waking them by having that doorbell ring again. Hurrying, she opened the door to find a man with a clipboard standing on her porch.

"Penny Oaks?" He had a bald head, bushy gray eyebrows, a tanned-to-leather face and broad shoulders.

"Yes…"

"Got a delivery for you," he said and thrust the clipboard at her. "Sign here."

"Sign for what?" Automatically she glanced at the delivery receipt. A furniture store? "What's this about?"

"Bring it all in, Tommy," the guy on her porch shouted before turning back to her. "I don't know what's going on. Just sign it, lady, and let me go back to the high life, okay?"

She did and then stepped back in astonishment as two more men unloaded a chocolate-brown leather sofa and matching chair.

"I didn't order that," she argued.

"Somebody did." The first guy just waved the paper at her. "We'll haul your old stuff away. Come on guys, got a million stops to make still."

"What're you—" She broke off as the two younger men smiled, nodded and slipped past her into her house. Then they were leaving, carrying her faded, overstuffed couch and chair out to the truck and then bringing in the new leather replacements.

Before she could ask any more questions, the truck pulled away and she closed the door, staring at new furniture she hadn't ordered.

"God, it smells as good as it looks," she murmured, walking to it to stroke the butter-soft leather as she would a cat. "But who— Colt. It had to be Colt," she assured herself. "He must have ordered it before he left. He probably forgot to tell me it was coming."

She sighed, sat on the arm of the couch and frowned when she heard the roar of a lawn mower starting up. Staring through her front window, she saw a gardening crew working on her lawn. *What was going on here?*

Before she made it to the front door, she heard the babies wake up and groaned. Apparently the sounds of the mower and the edger were too loud to sleep through. So much for naptime. She detoured to pick up her kids, plopping each of them on a hip, then went out onto the front porch.

"Excuse me!" she shouted to one of the guys using

a Weed Eater around the edge of her flower bed. "Who hired you?"

Reid wailed and screwed his eyes up, preparing to launch into a real scream, and once that happened, Penny knew Riley wouldn't be far behind.

"Really," she tried again, giving the hardworking man a hopeful smile. "I need to know…"

He waved and went back to work. At a loss for what to do next, Penny went back into the house, settled both kids on the floor near their toy box and then watched out the window while her yard was tidied.

"Your daddy's behind this, too," she whispered, feeling the sting of tears burn her eyes. "He won't stay, but he'll do this long-distance. Take care of my yard. Buy me new furniture. What's next?"

The doorbell rang and Penny stiffened. She hadn't actually expected an answer to that last question. Throwing a quick glance at the twins to make sure they were all right, she opened the front door to a man in a suit holding up a set of car keys.

"Who're you?" she asked.

"I'm just the messenger, ma'am," he said and handed the keys to her. "Enjoy!"

"Enjoy what?" Penny looked past him to see her fifteen-year-old reliable clunker being backed out of her driveway. "Hey! Wait!"

Panicking a little, she raced back to the living room, picked up the twins and then headed for the porch. The gardeners were already moving on to the backyard and there was a shiny red SUV parked in her driveway. From the corner of her eye, she saw her car making its slow, deliberate way down the street. "Wait! Come back!"

"I have come back," Colt said, stepping out from behind the SUV. "If you'll have me."

All the air left her body. Her stomach did a pitch and roll, then settled for butterflies. Thousands of 'em. Stunned speechless, Penny could only stare at him as he walked closer. Her gaze locked with his and her heart tumbled in her chest. "You're supposed to be on a volcano."

He gave her a quick grin that sent whips of electricity shooting through her veins.

"Now why would I want to do that when I could be right here?"

"Here?" She nearly choked on the word.

"Nowhere else," he said, stepping up onto the porch.

Penny held the babies, one on each hip, and laughed a little when they started bouncing and shrieking their delight at seeing their daddy again. Colt laughed, too, reached out and plucked both twins from her. He held them in his arms, kissed each of their foreheads and said, "I missed you guys."

"They missed you, too," Penny told him and surreptitiously wiped away one stray tear.

"How about their mother?" he asked. "Did she miss me?"

"A lot," she admitted, because what was the point of holding back now?

"Penny." His voice dropped to that low rumble that never failed to dance along her nerve endings like a caress. "You were right about me."

"What? Right? When?"

He smiled at her and said, "Can we go inside?"

"Yes. Sure." She stepped back and Colt slipped past her. He carried both babies into the living room, set them down with their toys, then came back to her. She couldn't look away from him. She was half afraid that if she did, he might disappear. That she was just having delusions or something because her heart had ached for him so badly.

But then he was there, in front of her. He smelled so good. His black hair fell across his forehead and his ice-blue eyes were—not icy at all, she realized. They were warm, like a sky in summer, and they were locked on her, showering her with emotions too dizzying to identify.

"You were right," he said softly, "when you said that I had been chasing death because I didn't want to risk living."

"Colt…"

He shook his head and grinned. "Don't lose your nerve now. Everything you said to me was right, Penny. But not anymore. I want to live. With you. With my kids. You guys are all I'll ever need."

Oh, God, she really wanted to believe him. But, "What about how you love adventure? How will you be happy living in a cottage in Laguna?"

He pulled her in for a quick hug, then set her back again so he could watch her eyes. So that *she* could read the truth in *his*. "Living with you and the twins and all of our other kids will be all the adventure I could ever need."

"All the—"

"And I know you love the cottage, but it's going to be way too small for the bunch of kids we're going to have, so I was thinking we could give the cottage to Robert and Maria and we could move to the cliff house?" Another smile. "If I live here, I'll eventually kill myself, you know, smacking my head into the low beams."

Her head was spinning. "All the kids we're going to have?"

"Caught that, huh?" His eyes were shining and his smile was wide. "We may even get another set or two of twins, who knows?"

"Another— Colt, you're moving too fast," she said. "I can't keep up." And, oh, how she wanted to.

"This isn't fast," he promised her. "I've wasted too much time already, thinking about the past instead of looking at the future."

He was right there with her. In her living room. Promising her everything. Looking at her with all the love she could have dreamed of, but he still hadn't said the words she needed to hear so badly.

"I talked to Con, too, before—"

"Before you hired a gardener, and bought me new furniture and a new car?"

"Exactly." He winked at her. "We're going to be restructuring our business. Con thinks it's a great idea. King's Extreme Adventures is going to become King's Family Adventures. We're going to find the best places for families to visit. To vacation. To experience the world. We want people to enjoy their lives, not risk them."

Her heart melted. "Oh, Colt…"

"Think about it! Way bigger customer base."

She smiled at him and could only think how happy she felt. How right it was to be here like this, with him.

"Con and I think you should take all the photos for the advertising, too.…"

"I think I need to sit down." Before she fell down. Afternoon sunlight spilled through the front windows and lay across the scarred wooden floors. Her kids were in the living room playing and giggling. And the man she loved was standing in front of her offering her the world and more.

"I'll hold you up," he promised, and wrapped his arms around her. "I swear to you, Penny, I will always be there for you. To depend on. To count on. I want you to feel like you can lean on me and let me lean on you. I won't ever let you down."

She stared up into his eyes, lifted one hand to cup his cheek and said, "I never believed you would, Colt."

He took a breath, pulled her in close and held on tightly. "We can talk about the business and the move and more kids right after I finish telling you the most important thing." He let her go, took a step back and dropped to one knee. "I'm doing it right this time."

Penny lifted one hand to the base of her throat and watched as her dreams became reality.

"I love you, Penny Oaks. I think I did from the very first moment I met you." He gave her a sad smile. "That's why I ran so far so fast. What I felt for you terrified me. Now, the only terrifying thing I can imagine is having to live without you." He pulled a jeweler's box from his pocket, flipped the velvet lid open and showed her a huge, canary-yellow diamond ring.

"Oh, Colt…"

"Marry me again, Penny. Share your life with me. I promise we'll have a great adventure."

"Yes, oh my God, yes, Colt. I will absolutely marry you!"

He jumped to his feet, swept her up into his arms and swung her in a circle before setting her down and sliding that ring onto her finger. Penny couldn't stop smiling.

"We'll have the kind of wedding you deserve this time," he said, cupping her face and pausing only long enough to kiss her senseless. "We'll have the biggest damn wedding California's ever seen. Anything you want."

She looked from the ring on her hand to the love shining in Colt's eyes and said, "All I want is to go back to the chapel where we were married the first time. Just you, me and the twins."

"God, you're amazing," he whispered and kissed her again. "I'll get the jet fueled. We can go tomorrow if your doctor says it's okay. Did you see him?"

"I did. He said I'm perfect."

Colt gave her a slow, wicked smile. "He's right about that."

Penny couldn't believe this was happening. She suddenly had everything she had ever wished for. The man she loved. Her children—

"Da!"

Penny and Colt went still and in tandem turned to look at the twins. Reid was standing on his own two feet and Riley clapped her hands and shouted again, "Da!"

He moved swiftly across the room, lifted both of the twins into his arms and just for a moment, buried his face in the sweetness of them. When he looked at Penny again, she saw *love* shining in his eyes.

"I can't believe I almost missed that," he whispered.

Penny walked to them, wrapped her arms around her family and held on. Until she heard another truck pull up out front. Pulling back, she eyed the man she loved warily. "What else did you do?"

Colt grinned and shrugged. "It's probably Rafe's crew to install a picket fence."

Laughing, Penny leaned into him and listened to the

steady beat of his heart. "I thought you hated picket fences."

"They're not so bad," he mused. "Besides, when the puppies get here, we'll need it."

"Puppies?" Shaking her head, she thought that life with Colton King would never be boring and she would always, always know what it felt like to be loved completely. Nothing could have been more perfect.

Colt bent his head, kissed her and whispered, "The adventure begins."

* * * * *

Don't miss these other BILLIONAIRES & BABIES *stories from*
USA TODAY *bestselling author Maureen Child:*

BABY BONANZA
HAVE BABY NEED BILLIONAIRE

All available now, from Harlequin Desire!

If you liked this BILLIONAIRES & BABIES *novel, watch for the next book in this number one bestselling Desire series,*
HIS LOVER'S LITTLE SECRET by Andrea Laurence, available April 2014.

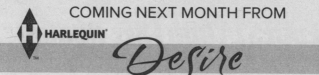

COMING NEXT MONTH FROM

HARLEQUIN®

Desire

Available April 1, 2014

#2293 ONE GOOD COWBOY
Diamonds in the Rough • by Catherine Mann
To inherit the family business, CEO Stone McNair must prove he isn't heartless underneath his ruthlessly suave exterior. His trial? Finding homes for rescue dogs. His judge? The ex-fiancée who's heart he broke.

#2294 THE BLACK SHEEP'S INHERITANCE
Dynasties: The Lassiters • by Maureen Child
Suspicious of his late father's nurse when she inherits millions in his father's will, Sage Lassiter is determined to get the truth. Even if he has to seduce it out of her.

#2295 HIS LOVER'S LITTLE SECRET
Billionaires and Babies • by Andrea Laurence
Artist Sabine Hayes fell hard for shipping magnate Gavin Brooks, and when it was over, she found herself pregnant. Now he's come to demand his son—and the passion they've both denied.

#2296 A NOT-SO-INNOCENT SEDUCTION
The Kavanaghs of Silver Glen • by Janice Maynard
The sexy but stoic Liam has headed the Kavanagh family since his reckless father's disappearance two decades ago. But meeting the innocent, carefree Zoe awakens his passions, derailing his sense of duty.

#2297 WANTING WHAT SHE CAN'T HAVE
The Master Vintners • by Yvonne Lindsay
Her best friend's last wish was that Alexis care for her baby—and her husband. So Alexis becomes the nanny, determined to heal this family without falling for the one man she can't have.

#2298 ONCE PREGNANT, TWICE SHY
by Red Garnier
Wealthy Texan Garret Gage promised to protect family friend Kate just as fiercely as her father would have. And he'd been doing just fine, until one night of passion changes everything.

HDCNM0314

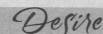
*A Wyoming business legend dies and leaves his nurse a
fortune. Now his son wants answers…*

"Colleen!"

That deep voice was unmistakable. Colleen had been
close to Sage Lassiter only one time before today. The night
of his sister's rehearsal dinner. From across that crowded
restaurant, she'd felt him watching her. The heat of his gaze
had swamped her, sending ribbons of expectation unfurl-
ing throughout her body. He'd smiled and her stomach had
churned with swarms of butterflies. He'd headed toward
her, and she'd told herself to be calm. Cool. But it hadn't
worked. Nerves had fired, knees weakened.

And just as he had been close enough to her that she
could see the gleam in his eyes, J.D. had had his heart attack
and everything had changed forever.

Sage Lassiter *stalked* across the parking lot toward her.
He was like a man on a mission. He wore dark jeans, boots
and an expensively cut black sport jacket over a long-
sleeved white shirt. His brown hair flew across his forehead
and his blue eyes were narrowed against the wind. In a few
short seconds, he was there. Right in front of her.

She had to tip her head back to meet his gaze and when she did, nerves skated down along her spine.

"I'm so sorry about your father."

A slight frown crossed his face. "Thanks. Look, I wanted to talk to you—"

"You did?" There went her silly heart again, jumping into a gallop.

"Yes. I've got a couple questions…."

Fascination dissolved into truth. Here she was, day-dreaming about a gorgeous man suddenly paying attention to her when the reality was he'd just lost his father. As J.D.'s private nurse, she'd be the first he'd turn to.

"Of course you do." Instinctively, she reached out, laid her hand on his and felt a swift jolt of electricity jump from his body to hers.

His eyes narrowed further and she knew he'd felt it, too.

Shaking his head, he said, "No. I don't have any questions about J.D. You went from nurse to millionaire in a few short months. Actually, *you're* the mystery here."

Read more of
THE BLACK SHEEP'S INHERITANCE,
available April 2014
wherever Harlequin® Desire and ebooks are sold.

HARLEQUIN®

Desire

ALWAYS POWERFUL, PASSIONATE AND PROVOCATIVE.

ONCE PREGNANT, TWICE SHY
Red Garnier

What's one impulsive night between old friends?

Tied together by tragedy, wealthy Texan tycoon
Garret Gage promised to protect family friend Kate
just as fiercely as her father would have. And he'd been
doing just fine until one night of passion and a secret
changes everything.

Look for
ONCE PREGNANT, TWICE SHY
by Red Garnier April 2014 from Harlequin® Desire!

Wherever books and ebooks are sold.

Also by Red Garnier
WRONG MAN, RIGHT KISS

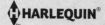

HIS LOVER'S LITTLE SECRET
Billionaires and Babies
by Andrea Laurence

She's kept her baby secret for two years...

But even after a chance run-in forces her to confront the father of her son, Sabine Hayes refuses to give in to shipping magnate Gavin Brooks's demands. His power and his wealth won't turn her head this time. But Gavin never stopped wanting the woman who challenged him at every turn. He has a right to claim what's his...and he'll do just about anything to prevent her from getting away from him again.

Look for HIS LOVER'S LITTLE SECRET
by Andrea Laurence April 2014, from Harlequin® Desire!

Don't miss other scandalous titles from the
Billionaires and Babies miniseries,
available now wherever ebooks are sold.

DOUBLE THE TROUBLE by Maureen Child
YULETIDE BABY SURPRISE by Catherine Mann
CLAIMING HIS OWN by Elizabeth Gates
A BILLIONAIRE FOR CHRISTMAS by Janice Maynard
THE NANNY'S SECRET by Elizabeth Lane
SNOWBOUND WITH A BILLIONAIRE by Jules Bennett